EDGE OF CREATION

THE GOD PARTICLE EXPEDITION

EDGE OF CREATION

THE GOD PARTICLE EXPEDITION

DOUGLAS RENDER

DEDICATION

To the dreamers and explorers
Those willing to imagine beyond today's existence
Be bold, take risks, find new adventures

HOW IT ALL BEGAN

If you are reading this, I have thrown off my imperfect shell and gone beyond human understanding.

This journal chronicles USS God Speed's odyssey through the cosmos, a voyage that took us to the far reaches of our solar system and beyond. We ventured into the depths of the Milky Way and the heliosphere in search of the God Particle.

Our mission began with visits to Luna Colony on the Moon and Ares Haven on Mars, both of which are vital outposts in humanity's quest to colonize space. These locations serve as critical stepping stones in our expansion beyond Earth, paving the way for future explorations and settlements.

During our transit to Mars, we received a distress call from the USS Bounty, a supply ship en route to Ares Haven Colony. They were stranded without engine power. Realizing we were the closest ship, we decided to divert from our course and provide assistance.

Launched a probe that successfully touched down on one of Jupiter's moons, Europa.

Made a short incursion into Uranus' atmosphere and deployed two probes.

Identified an asteroid traveling on an intercept course with God Speed, named Psyche. The team deployed a probe to learn more about Psyche and the minerals contained within.

Probes were sent into a debris field left by a passing meteorite, leading to the discovery of a new element. This added a new entry to the periodic table and revolutionized our understanding of elemental science.

The culmination of our travels was the pursuit of the elusive God Particle. A quest that could unravel the mysteries of the universe and redefine our understanding of fundamental physics.

With the aid of a newly developed propulsion drive, we exceeded the speed of light, thrusting God Speed into Transluminal space.

I have diligently recorded the exhilarating, perilous, and awe-inspiring experiences my team and I encountered.

Every entry strives to capture the essence of our expedition. I attempted to offer an unfiltered account highlighting the wonders and challenges unfolding among the stars. These words serve as a testament to the boundless spirit of exploration that drives humanity forward.

This is a humble tribute to the trailblazers of exploration —from the intrepid voyages of Magellan and Columbus to the pioneering expeditions of Lewis and Clark and the transcendent journeys of John Glenn and Neil Armstrong. It is a tribute to the unsung heroes, the tireless scientists, and technicians whose dedication quietly propels progress through the ages.

I inscribed these pages with profound honor, a testament to the collective spirit of humanity's relentless pursuit of knowledge. Tasked as one of the world's custodians of curiosity, entrusted with the quest to unravel the enigma of the God Particle.

KELVIN PASCAL

ASTROPHYSICISTS

CHASING THE GOD PARTICLE

May 15th, 2035

Sitting in my assigned rack, within the confines of our assigned berthing area, I begin documenting the most exciting adventure of my life with high expectations, unaware of what lies ahead for the team and me as we move through the expanses of space.

Throughout history, the question of a divine being's existence has sparked profound discussions and contemplation. It stands as a cornerstone of philosophical inquiry, delving into the essence of existence, purpose, and the nature of reality. *Is there a God? Is there only emptiness after death? How did the universe begin?*

Among the great debates lies the question of creation: did a supreme being fashion the universe, or did it come into being through the Big Bang? Some within the scientific community argue that both theories hold merit. As I reflect upon those scientists who came before me, many believed God or a God entity created the "God Particle", a single particle packed with sufficient energy to create the universe.

My entire life, I have been intrigued by the God Particle theory and its existence. It has caused me to contemplate: Is there a God who stands watch over his creation, deciding who will live, suffer, or die? *Did this entity create the God Particle?*

As C. S. Lewis presented in his writing "Miracles", does something exist outside of Nature, "the supernatural?"

I cannot reconcile this in my own mind. I have always believed in logic and science as the only surefire proof of life, and that once one has expired, their energy is absorbed into the universe. That is all.

The loss of my 13-year-old daughter from cancer two years ago re-enforced my belief that there is no God. My wife prayed every day, begging her God to save our daughter. Each day, the disease ravaged more of my little girl until it consumed her life. Where is this benevolent God?

So, I have endeavored to participate in this adventure. I will finally prove that God does not exist. Joining this expedition to find the God Particle will prove I am correct. There is no God or supreme being guiding mankind.

I know there have been well-known scientists who would disagree with my belief; Nicholas Copernicus, Galileo, Isaac Newton, Albert Einstein, and Erwin Schrodinger come to mind. Each acknowledged that something more significant than randomness contributed to the creation of the universe. At the end of this mission, we will see.

My mentor, Nobel Prize-winning physicist Peter Higgs, proposed the existence of the God Particle. He theorized that there must be a sub-atomic particle of a particular dimension that explains how other particles — and therefore all the stars and planets in the universe — acquire mass and become physical entities. This particle contained all the power necessary to bring life into existence, identified as the God Particle.

Soon, I will embark on this search with three of my colleagues, a military pilot, and a mission specialist.

These are the best of the best selected to ensure success on this monumental adventure.

Navy Captain: Buzz Albright – Pilot. A father of three, whose towering six-foot-five presence is matched only by the piercing depths of his cobalt-blue eyes. Within their gaze his a fusion of intelligence, mirroring the calm assurance of a seasoned spacecraft pilot. His stature alone instills trust. Affable and engaging, a perfect fit for the team.

Marine Corps Major: Juan Carlos—Mission Specialist. With his Marine crew cut, deep-set dark eyes, and a demeanor that manifests no-nonsense, Juan exudes an aura of unwavering confidence and competence. His mere presence instills a deep sense of confidence in those around him, assuring them that any obstacles on this adventure will be easily met and overcome.

Science Team Leader Astrophysicist: (me) Kelvin Pascal. I am a simple man striving to understand the relevance of our being. Since the death of my daughter, there has been an emptiness within my life that cannot be filled. A darkness that screams out in anguish, striving to understand that if God exists, why did he take an innocent child? I am searching for something more significant than human existence.

Condensed Matter Physicist - Vector Hawking. Small in stature, bald, with a look of consternation permanently plastered on his face, giving the impression he is constantly contemplating the world around him. Second cousin to Steven Hawking, Vector is driven to find his place in the science community, striving to step out of his cousin's shadow.

Atomic Physicist – Theo Venn. Affable. Easy to approach, always pleasant. His mind races from one topic to another with lightning speed, leaving others in the conversation scrambling to keep up. His enthusiasm for exploration and discovery is infectious, fueling an insatiable curiosity that knows no bounds. Engaging with him is like embarking on a whirlwind journey through a vast landscape of ideas, where each turn reveals a new vista to explore.

Molecular Physicist Gene A. Ray is wicked smart. In my estimation, she is the brightest member of the team. A physical fitness fanatic, she pushes the rest of the team to "keep moving." She is also one of the most pleasant members of the crew.

The success of our mission beyond the Milky Way hinges on the specialized equipment and expertise of each crew member. Their individual strengths and analytical prowess are indispensable for navigating the complexities of intergalactic travel beyond the speed of light in search of the God Particle.

With meticulous planning, each physicist has been assigned specific tools tailored to their expertise. This will ensure that our expedition is equipped to overcome any challenges encountered. Their collective knowledge and skill set are vital for unraveling the mysteries of the cosmos and achieving our objectives. Some of the equipment follows:

Neutron Star Interior Composition Explorer (NICER) measures X-rays emitted by neutron stars and other cosmic objects to help answer questions about matter and gravity.

Synchronous and free-electron lasers produce highly coherent light of wavelengths from the far infrared to hard X-rays; they identify nuclear material.

Utilizing sophisticated specialty computers, we can track radiation emissions from any power source entering the heliosphere.

Well, I will close. I am tired and it is late; tomorrow will be a busy day. We begin final preparation for launch.

FINAL PREPARATION

May 20th, 2035

Today was the final day of training in preparation for the launch, slated for June 1st. We spent the day reviewing launch procedures and simulations, running sophisticated scientific scenarios, to ensure everything was functioning nominally.

We had to perform some laser maintenance. The laser targeting mechanism for locating other crafts' docking ports must be re-calibrated. Juan informed us that If this failed to function properly, it would be difficult for our ship to dock with other craft. There had been incidents when failure resulted in collisions and damage to both ships.

Part of the day was a refresher course on navigating in a weightless environment. We climbed into our suits, which were surprisingly form-fitting and comfortable. We spent time in the weightlessness chamber. Halfway through the evolution, I got motion sickness. It was the first time since being in the program that this occurred. I hope it was an anomaly.

Next, we climbed into the simulator. The inside was an exact replica of our spacecraft. We were securely strapped into our seats in preparation for a simulated launch. A computer voice came over our communication system saying, "Standby for Launch." We were subjected to the same G-force felt in an actual launch. Vector slowly turned toward me, smiling and said, "I think I forgot to go to the bathroom before suiting up." The entire team laughed heartily, distracting us for just a moment. Suddenly, the G-force was gone.

We unstrapped ourselves and exited the simulator. The final evolution was to tour our home for the next few years. The ship has been christened "USS God Speed."

Our first stop was the main control room, where the ship would be piloted. The design engineer, Phil, pointed out features we were familiar with, except the artificial gravity selector. Phil placed his hand on the selector, saying, "This spacecraft is a pioneering marvel, the first of its kind to implement artificial gravity."

"Once God Speed enters space, this new technology enables the pilot to engage the artificial gravity system, transforming your weightless environment into one of familiarity. You will be able to walk around as if you were on Earth."

Phil-turned to us, laughing, and said, "This is the first of its kind, so be prepared to lose gravity at any time. We had issues with losing gravity during early testing, and the test crew would crash into the deck. All the bugs have been worked out, but since this will be the first go-live in space, you may want to hold on to something the first time it is engaged. Juan has been thoroughly trained to work through any problems that may be encountered."

God Speed was specially designed for extended space travel. It has sufficient space for each member to have a small private sleeping quarter, with a desk that folds out from the bulkhead. For eating and socializing, a table and chairs can be extracted from the deck with the touch of a button, enabling some comfort.

The scientific research area, situated aft, occupies one third of the craft. Throughout our journey, we will conduct a series of experiments and data collection initiatives, yielding invaluable insights that could significantly enhance future expeditions.

The galley, where we will eat, is located in the ship's center. With the capability of artificial gravity, we will be able to prepare meals as if on Earth. Microwave ovens will be the primary method for preparing meals.

Walking into the galley, to the left is the refrigerator, microwave, and counter for preparing meals. To the center are tables and chairs that can be stored beneath the deck plating with a push of a button.

At the forward section of the ship lies the main control center, where the pilot and engineer work in unison to navigate and manage the vessel's systems. Designed for efficiency and precision, this hub serves as the nerve center of the ship, ensuring smooth operation and rapid response to any challenges encountered in deep space.

The tour was the last evolution of the day. The crew disbursed to our berthing area.

As I sit here writing, I reflect on what some might call the ultimate quest—the search for the God Particle. As an astrophysicist, my life's work has been devoted to unraveling the universe's enigmatic origins. Mathematics has been the foundation of my understanding, reinforcing my belief that there is no God. I remain resolute in my atheism.

My journey is not solitary; it is shared with brilliant minds, each contributing unique perspectives and insights. Together, we will navigate the intersection of science and philosophy, enriching our understanding of the universe.

It will take fifteen years to reach our target, the Heliosphere. There, we will navigate the labyrinthine corridors of theoretical physics, forging new pathways and challenging established paradigms. The quest for the God Particle is a testament to our collective endeavor.

Our odyssey will not end there. It is a perpetual voyage of exploration fueled by an insatiable curiosity and an unwavering commitment to uncovering the mysteries of existence. Each hypothesis and experiment will bring us closer to an absolute understanding of the universe and our place within it. We hope to solidify all the years of personal sacrifice and work put forth by our team, culminating in the discovery of the God Particle.

Carl Sagan once said, 'Somewhere, something incredible is waiting to be known.'

As I reflect on this journey, I am reminded that exploration is not merely a pursuit—it is a promise to the universe that we will seek, question, and uncover its deepest mysteries. With boundless determination and an unyielding spirit of inquiry, we press onward, ever closer to the elusive truths that lie beyond the veil of the cosmos.

READY TO LAUNCH

May 30th, 2035

Tomorrow marks the commencement of a momentous voyage aboard the spacecraft God Speed alongside my esteemed colleagues. Departing from the illustrious launch pad in Florida at 0800 hours on June 1st, we will embark on a fifteen-year odyssey destined for the far reaches of the Milky Way. Our singular mission: to unravel the enigma of the God Particle, a pursuit that transcends individual aspirations, offering a glimpse into the profound mysteries of existence.

There is a theory among physicists; the Big Bang was not a random event. Rather a superior being, some call God with intent, created the universe. This creation began with one small powerful particle, named the God Particle. All the necessary power and elements were contained within this particle and once its creator initiated its expansion, the universe was created.

I feel the excitement of fulfilling a dream to be part of something greater than myself, maybe solving one of mankind's greatest mysteries. Many of our anxieties revolve around the unknown. We will be going further than any other human being has endeavored to go. There are no manuals, maps, or previous explorers we can lean on for guidance and inspiration. I consider this team Neo Magellan.

What if we fail to launch? What if we die along the way? What if there is nothing beyond the Milky Way?

In the face of such uncertainty, I reflect on the words of explorers and pioneers who came before us. They, too, faced the vast unknown without guarantees of success. Their courage and curiosity propelled humanity forward, and their legacy reminds us that the journey itself can be as significant as the destination.

As we embark on this extraordinary journey, I am filled with a profound blend of exhilaration and trepidation. Our mission is more than a scientific endeavor; it continues humanity's timeless quest to understand and explore the cosmos. I hope this expedition will ignite a spark of inspiration in others, just as the tales of past explorers once set my own passion ablaze.

To attempt this endeavor, a specialized Self-Guided Beam Propulsion drive was created. This new technology will propel us beyond the confines of light and into Transluminal space in hopes that the God Particle will be revealed.

I fear that at the age of thirty-five, knowing it will take thirty years for a round trip, I will die before making it back to Earth. Considering this possible outcome, I do not, for one moment, regret embarking on this adventure.

Carpe Diem!! We are off!

LAST ENTRY FROM EARTH

June 1st, 2035

    As I settle into my seat aboard the God Speed, awaiting the momentous launch, I feel compelled to pen what is my final entry from Earth.

    0500 – The team congregated in the astronauts' cafeteria, indulging in a simple yet hearty breakfast of eggs and bacon. The conversation was sparse, overshadowed by the gravity of the impending launch. Yet, beneath the surface tension, an undeniable sense of excitement lingered. A collective understanding of the risks we willingly undertake in pursuit of this extraordinary adventure.

    0545 - Stepping into the sterile confines of the clean room, the atmosphere crackled with a potent blend of anxiety and anticipation. The moment's weight hung heavy as we meticulously donned our space suits.

    At the far end of the room, our pilot, Buzz Albright, and mission specialist, Juan Carlos, sought to alleviate some of the tension with their lighthearted banter and infectious laughter.

    Buzz saw the tension in my eyes, walked over smiling, and with a light touch on my shoulder, said, "No worries, my friend, if the launch fails, you won't even know it." A burst of laughter engulfed the clean room, seeming to relieve the tension. My thought – Ya, really funny.

0800—Leaving the clean room, the ground crew escorted the team out of the building and into a secure van that took us to the launch pad. The van came to a stop a few feet from the elevator that transported us high above the surface to God Speed's entry hatch.

Looking out from a window inside the elevator, I was amazed at the contrasting sights: the ground was brown and desolate, with a beautiful blue sky in the background. Seeing this wondrous sight helped relieve my anxieties surrounding the flight.

As we exited the elevator, the flight manager guided us to God Speed's open hatch. Inside, we took our designated seats, the hum of the spacecraft's systems buzzing around us. The flight crew moved with practiced precision, tugging and securing our seat belts with methodical care, ensuring every strap was tight and secure for the upcoming launch.

Finally settled in, the flight manager asked, "How does that feel?"

Everyone on the team echoed a grunt of confirmation.

After the flight crew exited the craft, I watched as they closed and secured the hatch. There was a clank and a suction sound confirming that the hatch was secured and ready for launch. The silence at that moment was almost overwhelming. This was the moment everyone realized that all the time spent preparing for this mission was upon us; there was no turning back now.

Turing from one crew member to the other, I could see each lost in contemplation. I closed my eyes and saw my daughter's smiling face.

The silence was broken when Juan, chuckling, said, "Well, team, we are sitting on a fireball ready to either send us into space or oblivion." Everyone laughed, relieving the tension.

With each crew member securely strapped into our seats, we braced ourselves for the exhilarating journey ahead. As the countdown commenced, I couldn't help but feel the adrenaline coursing through my veins. If all goes according to plan, I'll have the opportunity to document our adventures in a new entry tomorrow. Until then, onward and upward.

Last thought, I hope I am strapped in tightly.

LIFT OFF

June 2nd, 2035

Yesterday, as God Speed strained to escape Earth's atmosphere, the pressure on my body was enormous. It felt as if three people were standing on my chest.

While rattling in my seat, I thought, "This is worse than any simulation we experienced during training."

I began to panic. My heart beat rapidly, and sweat beads were collecting in my helmet. Sitting next to me, Juan heard my anxious breathing, reached over and, with a deep, calming voice, assured me all was well. He laughed and said, "Enjoy the ride; it is better than an E-ticket at Disney World."

Shortly after we burst through the Earth's atmosphere, the engine's thrust diminished. Looking out the port window to my left, I was in awe of the sight before me: the deep, dark expanse of space, small twinkling stars, and the Moon shining brightly.

I saw the most amazing sight in my life. It took my breath away—Earth, a beautiful sphere of blue skies and white clouds shining against the blackness of space. It was surreal, and it was an excellent way to begin this adventure.

I watched in awe as the vast expanse of space before us seemed to come alive. It was a moment of realization—this was no longer just our mission. We were not alone. As Elon Musk has envisioned, a future where many ships set their sights on the stars felt tangible that day. No fewer than ten other craft surged away from Earth, their engines burning bright as they ventured into the unknown, each representing humanity's ever-growing presence in the cosmos.

There are colonies on the Moon and Mars; possibly, that is the ships' destination.

Buzz looked around, smiling, pressed his intercom button, and said, "Well, take off your seat belts, see how it feels to be without gravity."

I released my belt and slowly floated up like a helium balloon. We were like children, laughing, enjoying the experience.

After a few minutes, Buzz depressed his intercom button and said, "Alright, so much for fun. You may want to get into your seats. I am going to engage the artificial gravity."

He counted down, "Three, Two, One. One moment, we were floating in the vast expanse, and the next, gravity engaged, grounding us as if we were back on Earth's surface.

Juan hovered over the artificial gravity monitors to ensure proper functionality. After about ten minutes, Juan's voice came off the intercom, "Gravity is stable".

Buzz spoke, "Our next stop is the Moon. Based on our course and speed, we should arrive in three days."

We were tasked with stopping over to provide supplies to Luna Colony (Roman Goddess of the Moon). It was established in 2031 with a team of six scientists and a military support staff of three. The mission goal is to develop a viable, self-sustaining colony within five years.

Once we arrive, our orders are to spend two days assisting in completing a fusion power plant. This plant will enable the colony to generate sufficient power to support a large human community.

I'm excited about the prospect of reaching the Moon. I have an old friend there whom I have not seen in many years. She is part of the science team.

Day 1 in space – so far, so good.

THE MOON

June 4th, 2035

This morning, looking out of my window as we approached the Moon, its gray mass, pocked with holes created by meteors, reminded me how desolate this orb appears. It is smaller than I had imagined, but still impressive.

My first thought was, " Why *would anyone want to live on this lifeless orb?"* Considering minimal gravity, no air, and limited resources that need to be collected and converted into life-supporting material, it was not ideal for me.

Buzz's voice came over the intercom, jolting me from my thoughts, "All hands, prepare to receive the colony's supply ship. We are unloading supplies slated for Luna Colony."

Eager to observe the resupply process, I navigated through the ship's corridors until I reached a vantage point overlooking the docking bay.

Beyond the viewport, the supply shuttle drifted closer, its thrusters firing in short bursts to fine-tune its approach. A hush seemed to settle over the ship as the two vessels aligned, the delicate ballet of motion a testament to precision and control. With a soft thump, the shuttle made contact, a faint tremor resonating through the hull as the access hatch engaged.

A seamless connection—one more step in the endless rhythm of survival in the void.

A hollow sucking sound filled the corridor as the hatch creaked open, the telltale sign that atmospheric pressure between the two spacecraft had equalized.

The supply ship captain was first through the hatch. He reached out his hand toward Buzz saying, "Good morning, I am, Captain Jason Arganot, shuttle commander." Buzz shook Jason's hand with a huge smile, welcoming him aboard God Speed.

Turing and pointing at supply bundles laid out in the shuttle bay, Jason asks, "Are these ours?" Buzz nodded in acknowledgment. The supply transfer was accomplished within twenty minutes.

Just before reentering his ship, Jason turned to Buzz. "Captain, the science team has been eagerly awaiting these supplies. I understand your orders include sending your scientists to assist with the fusion project at the colony. A shuttle will be on standby tomorrow, ready to transport your crew to the surface. Just contact Launch Central when you're ready."

Buzz gave a firm nod. "Understood, Jason. I'll coordinate with my team and notify the colony."

With a final nod, Jason stepped into the airlock. As the hatch sealed behind him, Buzz reached for the intercom, opened the communication channel, "Team Luna Colony's administration has requested our scientists assist with the fusion power plant project. Once your work has been accomplished, there will be time for a tour of this unique facility. We will be the first guests to visit the colony. The shuttle will arrive early tomorrow morning. Take enough gear for a one-week stay."

Anticipation hung thick in the air. The colony's fusion initiative was a pivotal step toward energy independence, and the supplies they had just delivered would accelerate progress. While the scientists on the surface had been running simulations for months, hands-on expertise from our crew would be invaluable.

I am excited for this opportunity; my friend Elizabeth T. Snodgrass (Elmo) is assigned as a physicist to the colony. She is an old roommate and an extraordinary love. I gave her the nickname because she was sweet and cuddly like Elmo. We lost contact after college, each blinded by our ambitions, losing each other in the fog.

I look forward to our visit.

Before I go to bed, I will try to reach her by radio to confirm her availability and willingness to meet with me. She has been in the colony for five months.

Sitting at my port window, looking out at the beautiful orb of the moon, I grab my whiskey from the table, lift it to the sky, and take a sip. A toast comes to me: "Here's hoping the remainder of the trip will be as smooth as these first few days."

LUNA COLONY

LUNA COLONY

June 5th, 2035

I woke early in anticipation of our visit to the Moon's surface. Jumping quickly into the shower, shaved, dressed, and dashed to breakfast with the bounce of a child ready for his first trip to an amusement park. Not to mention seeing Elmo.

As a side note, God Speed is the first to install sonic showers. These showers utilize ultrasonic vibrations to remove dirt and grime from my body without the need for water. I simply step into the shower, activate the sonic vibrations, and emerge clean and refreshed.

Feeling sonic waves crashing on my body is less soothing than having warm, soapy water slowly washing away the day's grime.

This trip to Luna will be a nice break from our ever-present work, preparing to find the God Particle.

In anticipation of what would come, I almost ran to the embarkation shuttle bay. The rest of the team had beaten me. I smiled, saying, "Good morning, boy, what an exciting day!" Vector and Theo looked at each other and laughed. Gene smiled and said, "Well, I guess you have more incentive to go to the surface than we do." Everyone laughed. I realized they knew about Elmo. With red cheeks, I replied, "Well, let's get moving."

We climbed into our space gear, preparing to be picked up by the colony's shuttle. Looking out of the starboard hatch, I watched in amazement as the shuttle approached. It was the first of its kind. Sleek and aerodynamic, it looked more like a fighter jet than a transport. A crew of two or autonomously can pilot the craft. The autopilot had some glitches; the colony's leadership had elected to trust pilots until the bugs were worked out.

Standing near the docking port, I watched as the shuttle gracefully closed and engaged its clamps, securely connecting itself to the ship. I heard a vacuum sound and saw a green light illuminate above the hatch, confirming it was safe to open the access door. The hatch opened with a metallic clang, and the pilot stepped out and smiled, saying, "Welcome. I am Captain Cook. I am here to take you to the surface."

As I entered, I saw the craft was roomy, with sufficient space to accommodate ten passengers and cargo. There were two seats at the front of the craft for a pilot and co-pilot. The control panels were "touch screen."

This craft was the first to introduce voice-activated command and control. The pilot could issue voice commands to maneuver the craft instead of controlling the ship with the touch screens and steering console.

After slowly uncoupling from the God Speed, the pilot squawked over the intercom, "Hang on. Now the fun begins." He chuckled and said, "Hold on to your hats."

The engines fired quickly, thrusting the craft forward and throwing me back into my seat. The G-force was less than when we exited Earth's orbit, but still an exciting experience.

Sure, wish the pilot had given us a better heads-up about how powerful the craft was. But, considering the double warning, I should have been prepared.

After catching my breath, I settled for the thirty-minute transit to the planet.

As we entered the Moon's atmosphere, the pilot said, "I am going to turn the landing over to our computer, Rachel. No worries, if a problem arises, I am at the controls and can override her."

The pilot turned to his console, chuckling, and said, "Ok, Rachel, take us home."

A soft, soothing voice replied, "Colt, I have it from here. Just set back and enjoy the ride."

Descending to the Moon's surface was an exhilarating experience that left us in awe. The ship smoothly transitioned into a five-degree angle as we pierced through the exosphere. Inside the cockpit, the pilot's voice remained calm as he said, "Rachael, remember to adjust to the new safe descent angle."

Rachael's soft, reassuring voice replied, "Now, Captain, you know how smooth I am."

Piercing through the atmosphere, I could see the outline of the colony.

Suddenly, an unexpected shift occurred. The pilot's tone tightened. His commands grew urgent as Rachael failed to respond.

Anxiety gripped us as the ship veered into a downward spiral, hurtling us towards the surface below and a certain death. Because of the change in the angle of our descent, flames could be seen on the outer hull, caused by increased friction.

At that moment, the possibility of our odyssey ending before it began loomed large. I chuckled and smiled, speaking into my intercom, "Well, if there is a God, I will see him without finding the God Particle. " The team burst into a great outburst of laughter.

Laughing, Gene replied, "I should have rubbed Buddha's belly before we left."

This caused a great uproar of laughter.

With a sudden jolt that threatened to wrench our seats from their moorings, the pilot took back control from Rachael. The ship stabilized into a smooth glide, relief flooding through us as we realized we had narrowly averted disaster.

Over the intercom, the pilot's voice crackled, laced with humor, "Well, that was interesting. I guess we need a little more tweaking on Rachael's control. How's the ride so far?" Laughter filled the cabin in shared relief, grateful to be alive.

Juan responded, "Well, I don't know about the rest of you, but I am glad I went to the bathroom before leaving."

Approaching the landing zone, the shuttle maneuvered gracefully, akin to a Harrier jet's capability to land vertically. The ship gradually slowed its forward thrust until it came to a gentle, vertical landing. The craft's ability to launch and land vertically proved invaluable, particularly for navigating the Moon's unstable surfaces.

Peering out of the shuttle window, we saw an astounding sight: three interconnected domed structures nestled within a crater, which had been designated "Amundsen Rim."

Each building was framed with intricate hexagonal architecture. The structures were built ten meters deep into the crater, with their rounded contours blending seamlessly with the lunar landscape. Building the structures into the crater protected the colony from violent weather and overexposure to radiation.

We quickly detached from our seats and migrated to the exit. The colony leadership stood on the tarmac and welcomed us as the first guests to this scientific marvel.

Elmo stood in the background, smiling and waving for me to come to her. I moved quickly to her, smiled, reached out with both arms, and embraced her tightly. What a wonderful feeling. Untangling from the embrace, Elmo said, "My friend, it has been a long time. I am so happy to see you." She pointed toward a building, saying, "Let's be on our way to my quarters for a drink and to catch up."

Once we were safely inside and had shed our gear, I turned to Elmo—and for a moment, I was utterly mesmerized. Age had done nothing to diminish her beauty. Her long, dark hair, almond-toned skin, and unforgettable blue eyes were exactly as I remembered. The sight of her stole my breath.

This was my first night on Luna Colony, and it was exciting. After catching up and having a whiskey, Elmo gave me an extensive tour of the colony.

I was intrigued to see how Luna had been built and what science had been used to ensure sufficient water, air, and food supplies.

I am at peace with this distraction. I am spending time with Elmo and assisting with bringing the fusion power plant online.

The God Particle mission can wait.

LUNA COLONY DAY 2

June 6th, 2035

Earlier this evening, as I sat with Elmo, sipping whiskey beneath the dim glow of the lights in her quarters, my thoughts drifted to the God Speed science team. Their contributions to the Colony's fusion power plant had been nothing short of trans formative. I had known they were talented—but their brilliance, depth of knowledge, and precision had far surpassed even my highest expectations.

The Luna Colony team took two years to build the plant's infrastructure. Power lines had to be run from the plant and connected to the main circuits. Switching mechanisms were installed to enable a smooth transition from solar panels as the primary power source to the fusion power plant.

This morning, I walked through a small passageway from the staff berthing pod into the main cafeteria. Vector, Gene, and Theo sat with Luna's scientists, who shared their experiences and challenges building the Colony.

Looking to my left, Elmo was ordering her breakfast. I slid beside her, bent down, and whispered, It was excellent spending time with you last night. With a twinkle in her eye, she turned and smiled, saying, "It's been a long time." She was handed her breakfast order, turned, and headed for the scientist's table.

I ordered eggs and bacon, grabbed my plate, and joined the team.

Vector stood looking at me and said, "There is a briefing in the conference room in ten minutes. Looks like you will have to gobble those eggs quickly. That's the price you pay for having company last night." Everyone laughed as they looked at Elmo. Her face flushed as she smiled sheepishly.

I quickly consumed my breakfast, grabbed coffee, and headed for the conference room. The walk from the cafeteria was short. Looking up through the solar-plated windows, I could see the beautiful blue orb of Earth.

This engineering marvel is plate glass infused with solar collectors, which supply all the Colony's power needs. The pod structures were perfectly designed, each linked together, allowing movement from berthing to any other part of the Colony without needing to suit up and go outside.

The solar array generates significant power to support day-to-day operations. Except during Lunar storms, the panels become coated with sand, reducing the amount of energy that can be collected.

This results in brownouts, as the computer system prioritizes where the power must be distributed. We experienced this today as we walked to the conference room. The lighting dimmed for a short period of time.

The Colony's leadership believes that once the fusion power plant becomes operational, it will generate more power than the current infrastructure requires, thereby alleviating these issues. The plant will enable Luna to receive more personnel, moving closer to human consciousness, to thrive beyond Earth.

Entering the conference room, I sat down next to Elmo. She turned and smiled a devilish smile, remembering the night we had together. She reached under the table and gently squeezed my knee. I smiled, placed my hand on her thigh, and held it during the entire briefing. Her soft, supple leg reminded me of our time together.

We were briefed on the Colony's ambitious plan to initiate the fusion power plant. Vector and Theo, with their extensive knowledge of Helium-3 and deuterium, were assigned to collaborate with Luna scientists.

The process of combining deuterium and Helium-3 releases a large amount of energy in the power plant.

Dr. Lucien Volt, the scientist in charge of this project, looked at me smiling. "Kelvin, if you can pull yourself away from Elmo, I am assigning you and Gene the task of switching over the power from the solar array to the fusion power plant. This must be accomplished at the primary circuit once the fusion plant is placed online."

Red-faced, I looked at Dr. Volt and could only nod, confirming I understood my assignment.

Our role was to wait for radio authorization from Dr. Volt to throw the switch, which would change the primary power source to the fusion power plant.

Gene smiled reassuringly and remarked, "No task is too small when we're propelling Luna Colony into a new era of limitless power."

The briefing was adjourned. Gene and I made our way to the primary exit hatch and donned our protective gear. The suit felt snug and secure, its layers shielding us from the harsh environment outside the facility.

Turning to the exit hatch, I radioed to the control room, "We are preparing to enter the air lock, decompress, and exit the launch bay."

I closed the airlock hatch behind me and pressed a red button on the bulkhead labeled "decompress and exit." Suddenly, I heard a hissing sound as the room's atmosphere equalized to that of the moon.

Air slowly vented from the airlock over several minutes. My suit puffed up slightly as the external pressure dropped. I walked to the exit hatch and pressed the "open" button. A metallic click could be heard, and the outer door slowly opened into the Moon's surface. A foreboding, gray, desolate environment was before us.

We were now stepping into the pure vacuum of space. No wind or pressure could be felt, utter silence. The light was incredibly sharp. I quickly flipped down my protective visor.

Gene and I began our trek towards the Colony's primary circuit. The silence was punctuated only by our breathing and the occasional crackle of static from the comms.

I looked at Gene and said, "Watch." With the surface's gravity 1/16 of Earth's, I jumped into the air and began bouncing. Gene laughed and began to do the same. I felt like a kid, enjoying the thrill. We quickly covered the distance to the primary circuit.

The primary circuit is a complex technology web critical to our mission's success. We reached our destination and began the final checks, ensuring everything was in place for the moment we would activate the switch.

Time ticked by as we waited for confirmation to throw the switch. Three hours after arriving on station, Dr. Volt's voice finally cracked over our radio: "Kelvin, it is a go to perform the switch over."

My reply was filled with excitement. I realized we were contributing to advancing Luna Colony's ability to populate the Moon. Roger, I will radio once the switch has been thrown."

Standing next to the panel, "Ready?" Gene asked, her voice steady despite the tension.

"Ready," I confirmed, focusing on the task that could determine the fate of Luna Colony's future. I reached up with both hands and grunted, pulling down the converter switch.

Suddenly, the entire compound went dark. I reached down and pressed the transmission button on my radio. With worry evident in my voice, I ask, "Dr. Volt, we have gone dark. What is the problem?

After a prolonged silence, Dr. Volt responded, "Kelvin, everything's under control here. One of the primary circuit boards is faulty. The team is working to fix it. Switch the circuit back to solar power. We'll notify you once the issue is resolved. Right now, we urgently need power for critical oxygen systems."

Gene activated her headlamp, illuminating the central circuit console. I swiftly reached out and toggled the converter switch. Darkness gave way to light throughout the Colony. With relief, I keyed my mic, reporting, "Dr. Volt, systems are stable here. Standby for authorization to switch over Power."

Two hours after our last communication, Dr. Volt's voice came excitedly over the radio, "Kelvin, it took some time to replace the board. We are good to go."

Gene smiled and nodded, reached out, and pulled down the converter switch. The lights flickered. My first thought was, "Here we go again, no power." Slowly, throughout the colony, lighting began to glow brighter than when powered by the solar panels. The solar array had been stressed, causing occasional brownouts throughout the Colony.

Turning to Gene, I remarked, 'Well, we have sufficient power now. Hopefully, no more brownouts.'"

When we entered the conference room for our post-implementation analysis, the air buzzed with excitement. Scientists from the colony animatedly discussed their plans for utilizing the newly established power sources.

Despite the minor board failure, the implementation proceeded smoothly.

Now, equipped with a fusion plant and a solar array, the colony is well on its way to sustainability. The fusion plant will be the primary power source, marking a crucial step toward establishing a permanent lunar settlement.

The solar array will provide supplementary power as needed and be a backup during fusion plant maintenance.

Sitting in my berthing area, completing this evening's entry, I am overjoyed with the Colony's success. With Elmo's company, I am more content than one could imagine. She is an excellent companion, one that will be sorely missed.

We will be departing for our next adventure tomorrow.

One final night with Elmo. I will miss her again.

DEPARTING LUNA COLONY

June 7th 2035

Today marked our return to God Speed, signaling the resumption of our odyssey after a welcome respite on Luna Colony—a much-needed relief from the routine of shipboard life since departing Earth.

The first leg of our adventure, Earth to the Moon, required a two-day transit. It will take nine months to reach Mars. This will be the longest time we will spend together on God Speed. I wonder how well we will do in the confined space for that length of time.

Fortunately, the craft has many amenities to occupy our idle hours. We have access to a comprehensive exercise facility, an extensive video and reading library, and a diverse array of video games. Theo and Vector will dedicate most of their off-duty hours to their passion: video games.

Buzz and Juan love sporting events. They will be able to see delayed transmitted games. We are one of a few spacecraft outfitted with a state-of-the-art communication platform that employs laser beams to transmit all audio and video communications. These transmissions are directed from the ship towards laser relay stations strategically positioned in space, with most stationed in orbit around designated planets.

It is truly remarkable how efficient communication over vast distances has become with lasers.

My time spent with Elmo was particularly cherished. She is an avid soccer fan. Last night, we watched a World Cup game. It was great fun.

Last night, as we lay next to one another, we couldn't shake the realization that this might be our final encounter in the realm of the living. She has been my friend since our university days, and we have always shared a unique bond. Our friendship blossomed in academia, where we pushed each other to excel in our studies, constantly striving to be the best versions of ourselves.

We reminisced about our college days, living together, and the great fun we had in each other's company. When our eyes met, a warm feeling consumed me. I realized in that moment my passion for her had never dwindled. Sadly, I looked away, feeling uneasy, this unexpected reaction to her presence. With a twinkle in her eye, Elmo smiled and spoke, "You know I have never loved anyone but you; we put our careers ahead of all else. I have come to realize it is a lonely place to be."

I placed my arms around her, pulled her close, and comforted her.

At that moment, the thought crossed my mind: Well, if the God particle exists, maybe there is a God, and just maybe I will see her on the other side. Until then, we charge into the breach!!

Before I knew it, morning had come, and we were back on God Speed.

Elmo's exceptional ability to quickly analyze and solve scientific challenges makes her an invaluable asset to the Moon project. Her keen intellect and unwavering determination have been instrumental in overcoming many obstacles. It's no surprise that she has risen to such prominence in our field.

Thanks to the advanced communications array, I will be able to stay connected with Elmo through video chats. These virtual meetings will be a lifeline, allowing us to share our thoughts, ideas, and feelings despite our physical distance. I will miss my friend.

Contemplating my age and the vast expanse of time required to traverse to the heliosphere, I'm confronted with the sobering possibility that I may not endure our return journey. Such thoughts weigh heavily upon me as we prepare to embark on the next leg of our expedition.

Luna Colony emerges as a marvel of scientific ingenuity, nestled beneath the protective embrace of its glass dome structures. These domes shield the colony from the harsh lunar environment and are infused with transparent solar panels, capturing and converting sunlight into vital energy. Their honeycomb design imparts resilience and elegance to the colony's architecture, a testament to meticulous engineering.

A monumental leap forward comes with the activation of Luna Colony's pioneering fusion power plant—the first of its kind. Until now, it had been a scientific theoretical ambition. With our assistance, Luna's scientists now have a process in place to extract helium-3 from the Moon's surface. Infusing deuterium with Helium-3 generates power within the plant.

Surpassing all expectations, this revolutionary facility yields abundant energy, far exceeding current needs. With its inauguration, the colony's horizon expands, promising to construct additional structures and heralding the imminent arrival of civilians. It marks the genesis of a new civilization, unfurling its roots on the lunar surface.

This is one step closer to fulfilling Elon Musk's ambition to perpetuate mankind's consciousness beyond Earth. He believes that sooner or later, man will destroy Earth, and without an alternative planet, Human consciousness will be gone.

Buzz has been directed to obtain a copy of all data from this program and deliver it to Mar's Ares Haven. Ares has the necessary building materials to construct a fusion plant, and with the data we are carrying, Ares will be able to bring its fusion power plant online.

One technical concern remains. Current research indicates the amount of Helium-3 on Mars's surface is a little more than Earth's. This could cause the fusion project to fail before it begins.

At the heart of Luna's sustainable ecosystem lies the Hydroponic Bay, a nexus of life and innovation. Here, lush greenery thrives, nourishing the colony's inhabitants. Yet, its significance transcends mere sustenance. Within its confines, carbon dioxide, exhaled by the colony's inhabitants, is repurposed as the verdant flora absorbs it. In return, the bay exhales oxygen, completing a vital cycle of life support.

Luna Colony's resourcefulness knows no bounds. Gray water, gleaned from the Moon's surface, is repurposed to bolster the Hydroponic Bay's operations. This meticulous extraction and recycling process epitomizes the colony's commitment to maximizing every available resource, ensuring a harmonious coexistence with its lunar home.

Oxygen is also extracted and piped into the facility during the gray water conversion process.

In the quiet expanse of space, Luna Colony stands as a beacon of human achievement, a testament to our boundless ingenuity and unwavering spirit of exploration. It represents a settlement and a harbinger of a future where humanity thrives among the stars.

I departed Luna somewhat melancholy, knowing there may never be another opportunity to see Elmo again in this world.

Tonight's sleep will be uneasy.

ON TO MARS

June 8th, 2035

This morning, standing in my berthing, looking out the portal, drinking a fresh cup of coffee, I watched the Moon shrink from my view as God Speed propelled us to Mars.

I stood in wonder, thinking about the marvels of science that enable human survival in such a hostile environment. It never ceases to astound me.

It's a testament to the dedication of every scientist and technician who paved the way for those now calling the Moon home.

I'm eager to learn about the progress on Mars. Ares Haven Colony, established just a year ago, holds immense promise despite encountering challenges in maintaining its power grid.

Mar's sandstorms present a constant problem, covering the solar array. This requires constant clearing. The crucial data we possess will enable Ares to develop its own fusion nuclear power plant. This fills me with hope.

The Colony has begun constructing the power plant, which should be completed prior to our arrival. Efforts to collect Helium-3 are underway. Once the Helium-3 conversion process is implemented, the facility stands ready to power up, revolutionizing living conditions on the red planet.

Vector's expertise, honed on the lunar surface alongside the Luna team, is invaluable. His deep understanding of fusion power will undoubtedly expedite the implementation of a stable energy source on Mars. This will ensure the colony's sustainability and growth.

It's remarkable to witness the seamless collaboration between minds across celestial bodies, all united to expand humanity's consciousness beyond Earth. Humans are the most destructive beings created. Without expanding beyond Earth, humankind will cease to exist. We are destroying our only habitable planet. Sometime in the near future, Earth will be destroyed.

As I work and spend time with crew members, I better understand who and what they are about.

Theo is an interesting character; his interests beyond science are varied. He has entertained us on many evenings, playing the piano and singing, and is also a master at the card game Bridge. While playing, he can be heard boasting, "If not for his love of science, I would have been a world-class bridge player. He is quite the athlete. Well, if you call Canadian, curling a sport. How much effort and exertion is expended to stand on the ice, grab a round stone with a handle, and slide it down into a set of circles? Similar to shuffleboard. I ask him why he likes an old folks' game. He sneered, laughed, and said, "We drink a lot of beer when we play."

Theo and I spent the better part of the day observing stars and planetary moons, utilizing a telescope similar to, but on a smaller scale than, the Webb telescope. Our task was to review our plotted course and make any adjustments to ensure the most direct route to the heliosphere, which would be uneventful.

Peering into the vast expanse beyond the Milky Way, my mind drifted, pondering the mysteries awaiting us on our cosmic odyssey. My thoughts turn to Ulysses and his legendary ten-year voyage homeward. Trials and tribulations beset him as he sought to reunite with his beloved wife and homeland of Ithaca.

Like Ulysses' voyage, home and his uncharted path, we enter our own uncharted waters, not knowing what challenges lie ahead for us. Might we encounter the celestial equivalent of Ulysses' trials – errant comets veering dangerously close, enigmatic anomalies forcing us off our intended course? And crucially, can we muster the resolve and ingenuity to navigate these obstacles and emerge victorious? Does the God Particle exist?

Theo and I spent the evening sitting in the lounge area, drinking whiskey, and watching the never-ending bleakness of space, mesmerized by the nothingness. We discussed our families and friends, wondering how they were doing back on Earth. In these moments, the vastness of space seemed to shrink, and the bonds between us grew stronger.

It is late, and I must rest to ensure that I am at my best for tomorrow.

Even Ulysses, for all his trials, found moments of peace beneath the stars. May my team's sleep be deep, their dreams untroubled, and strength renewed for whatever awaits on the horizon. Tomorrow is a blank page.

THE RED PLANET

February 7th, 2036

We are six days out from Mars. Watching the red planet grow larger each day is both fascinating and unsettling. The idea of supporting a large, thriving population on such an inhospitable world is almost beyond comprehension. I remain skeptical that it can be done. With its searing heat, brutal cold, and near-total lack of atmosphere, one has to wonder: why would anyone choose to live there?

A small group of scientists from the U.S., England, France, and Japan have volunteered to take on this huge undertaking. Their mission is to determine whether the planet has sufficient resources to sustain life.

During our daily briefing, the monotony was abruptly shattered by the blaring of an alarm from our long-distance sensors. Quickly moving to the equipment console, Buzz reviewed the incoming data.

Returning to the briefing, he informed the team that, based on the data, we would soon encounter an asteroid traveling near our projected trajectory toward Mars.

We discussed the possible implications and scientific value of this encounter. Everyone began speaking at once;

most believed this was a unique opportunity to monitor, track, and possibly explore the asteroid.

With a tone of excitement, Gene stood and said, "I recommend creating a plan to collect as much information as possible on this asteroid. We should consider landing a probe on its surface. Our probe, Hermes, was designed for such a purpose. What else would we be doing? Just flying?"

Vector bellowed out, "Come on! This will be another distraction from our primary objective. I want to prove to those who believe in the God Particle that it doesn't exist. It is a waste of our time to do this."

Gene turned to Vector and growled, in a sardonic voice, "Vector, you are a sad, selfish man, unwilling to see beyond your own thoughts. You are not the smartest person in the room, as you may believe."

Vector chuckled and smirked, "Decide what you will. I am having no part of this. It will be a colossal waste of time."

Gene slowly looked around the room, linking eyes with each team member and asking, "Well, do we act like scientists and take advantage of this once-in-a-lifetime opportunity? We could be like Vector, skulking in a corner, and be on our way."

Vector stood, stormed out of the briefing room.

Buzz shook his head as Vector disappeared. "Well, that was interesting. If we are going to study the Asteroid, let's start planning now."

Crafting a plan became our immediate focus, ensuring readiness to divert our course if necessary and to strategically develop the best approach for collecting data. This was a welcome distraction from the routine that had settled in after nine months of travel. Before this asteroid discovery, boredom had begun to settle in throughout the ship, and tension between crew members was palpable.

The other day, a conversation between Theo and Juan—stemming from their contrasting beliefs regarding the existence of the God Particle—escalated into a fistfight. It began in the galley while we were eating lunch. The discussion became heated when Theo insisted that the God Particle was only a theory. There is no relevant scientific evidence supporting its existence. He argued that religious-minded, fanatical scientists perpetuated the God Particle theory.

Juan, visibly agitated, stood, sliding back his chair, and said, "Theo, you fool, God does exist. You will see when we reach the Heliosphere and exceed the speed of light. As an atheist, you'll probably burn up when the God Particle appears."

Theo laughed mockingly, stood up, and shook his head, responding, "All you religious nuts are the same. Oh! God will save me!"

Before anyone could react, Juan leaped over the table, tackled Theo, and held him down with one hand while violently landing multiple punches to Theo's face.

It took three of us to drag Juan off of Theo. Theo stood up, clutching his nose as blood ran down his face from a broken nose.

Buzz raised his voice, saying, "Okay, everyone, get to the consoles and start brainstorming plans for exploring the asteroid. Theo, head to the medical bay and get your nose fixed."

An hour after the galley incident, we met in the conference room to discuss the best plans for exploring the asteroid. We agreed to land on the asteroid's surface with our specialized data collection probe, Hermes. Excited chatter enveloped the room as everyone postulated what we might find.

The probe was modeled after NASA's Perseverance. Within the NASA probe's cargo bay, a vehicle named Rover was utilized to traverse Mars. Rover mapped and collected samples from Mars in 2021. This research vehicle and the data collected contributed to identifying the best location to establish a Mars colony, Ares Haven, in 2033.

Our version of Perseverance, christened Hermes—the messenger of the gods—boasts numerous upgrades from its predecessor, including enhanced spectrometers, cameras, and lasers. These upgrades enable Hermes to search for organics and minerals altered by watery environments.

One of its most significant improvements is the ability to drill three meters into the surface to collect samples. Once the collection parameters have been met, Hermes will autonomously set a course back to God Speed, where we will thoroughly analyze the collected samples.

The team's speculations about the asteroid's mineral composition ran rampant, fueling our anticipation for a closer look. As scientists, such opportunities for up-close exploration are what drive us—the chance to unravel the mysteries of the cosmos one discovery at a time.
Will we discover living microbes and new minerals adding to the periodic table? My mind wandered.

We left the briefing room, slowly moving to our berthing for the night.

As I lie here, surrounded by the quiet of the night, I'm struck by the insignificance of humanity against the backdrop of the cosmos. The vastness of space renders our existence minuscule, a humbling realization that prompts reflection on our collective purpose. Who am I, and what should I be doing with the limited time that I have on this plane?

In the face of such cosmic grandeur, it seems trivial to cling to petty disputes and divisions among cultures, knowing that Earth is our lifeblood for now. Perhaps it's time for humanity to unite and find common ground in the vastness of space before we irreversibly destroy our only home.

I look forward to our visit to Mars. I expect to see something smaller and more primitive than the Luna Colony.

Our expertise in fusion power plants and the fusion data from Luna Colony should greatly improve the quality of life in this desolate outpost.

Pausing at this moment of reflection, thoughts of Elmo came rushing to the forefront of my mind. An emptiness overcame me, and I felt alone in the vastness of space. Once this mission to the Heliosphere has been accomplished, I am resolved to track down Elmo and dedicate the remaining days of my life to her.

In closing, I think of an old phrase my first mentor said to me as I was overwhelmed, postulating a theory I had. He stopped me mid-babble and said, "Kelvin, still your mind remember deeds, not words, win the day." Facta non verba.

ARES HAVEN

MARS

March 4th, 2036

Today was the day we would arrive at Mar's Ares Haven Colony.

As we approached and began our orbit, it looked more inhospitable than I had observed during our transit. Red sand everywhere, small dust storms cropping up, sometimes turning into full-blown tornadoes, ravaging everything in its path. It will be interesting to see how the science teams are thriving under these arduous conditions.

In our morning briefing, Buzz informed us that a supply ship would arrive to collect supplies we had onboard for the Colony. This must be accomplished before we would be able to go down to the surface.

Juan was assigned to coordinate the supply transfer. He met the craft after docking and directed the crew to the supply hold. Having waited two years for these supplies, the Mars crew's excitement and urgency to collect their booty and return to the surface were palpable.

One of the ship's crew, carrying a box labeled "potatoes", walked past me with a huge smile. He looked at me, saying, "Boy, it has been a year since I tasted potatoes."

Walking away, I could hear him listing the types of potatoes he was going to eat. "Mashed, baked, scalloped, boiled, and my favorite, French fries." He gleefully blathered.

The Mar's team wore giant smiles and shook hands with all of the crew they encountered. Buzz piped in Beethoven's Fifth Symphony and Journey's "We Are the Champions" to further enhance the mood.

Three hours later, Mar's supplies were loaded onboard the supply ship. There was a minor glitch when the craft decoupled from God Speed.

The supply ship pilot began moving away from us before the uncoupling had been accomplished. I was in the galley and felt a slight jarring. My coffee crashed to the deck. It felt as if we were being towed. Alarms were blaring, red lights flashing. Juan could be heard over the radio screaming, "Hold your position; you are not uncoupled. Stop!! You will tear a hole in my ship!"

Our team rushed to the bay, not knowing how bad the damage might be. Juan, standing looking through the hatch port window, could be heard screaming at the pilot over his radio, "Slowly inch back into the docking sleeve, the coupling joint failed to release." Holding our collective breath, we watched as the ships connected with an audible thud.

Everyone standing there felt the two ships merge. A sucking sound was heard, which confirmed there was an airtight seal between the two craft. Juan opened the hatch between the ships. He quickly began inspecting the seals and confirmed all was well.

He used a few robust expletives to make his point to the pilot that his error could have scrubbed our mission. The pilot apologized for his carelessness and promised to buy Juan a drink when he reached the surface.

After a short discussion with Juan, the pilot reentered his ship. The craft uncoupled, turned toward Mars, hit its boosters, and disappeared into the Martian atmosphere.

Buzz depressed the on switch to the ship-wide communication system. He laughed sardonically, saying, "Well, that was interesting. Crew, get into your gear and meet at our shuttle bay for transport to the Ares Haven. One can hope the rest of the Ares team are more conscientious than their pilot. Buzz's comment brought great laughter among the team.

We boarded our shuttle and headed for the colony. Juan remained on board to maintain God Speed, saying, "I need time alone without interruption to get my girl in shape for our next challenge."

After entering Mars's atmosphere, we headed for the North Pole, where Ares Haven was located. This site had been chosen for its ice packs, which could be converted to potable water and extracted oxygen. The area also contained natural resources, carbon dioxide, iron, aluminum, silicon, and sulfur, which were being converted to glass, bricks, and plastic. The planet's hydrogen and methanol could be combined to create fuel.

As we approached the Martian colony, the first thing that caught my eye was that it was much smaller than Luna Colony. Nestled within a vast crater, four imposing structures stood connected by intricate tubes, forming a network that allowed the crew to traverse safely from one building to another. It reminded me of gerbil habit trails. These structures were a testament to human ingenuity, showcasing the pinnacle of engineering achievement in the unforgiving Martian terrain.

I noticed most of the structures' roof solar panels, exposed to the Mars environment, were blanketed with Mars's rust-red sand. I was certain frequent maintenance is required to ensure proper exposure for the solar panels.

I wondered how efficient the solar panels were at collecting power to sustain the Ares team.

Among the structures, next to what appeared to be staff housing, stood a huge machine identified as a housing a 3D printer. We were informed it is the first of its kind—a scientific wonder.

This autonomous module was pivotal as one of the pioneering pieces of equipment to touch down on Martian soil. Its purpose? To fabricate all the environmentally sustainable structures comprising the Ares Haven Colony. Every building I saw was built using a 3D printer.

The module utilized Martian resources ice, calcium oxide, and indigenous rocks, employing cutting-edge technology to synthesize cement, laying the foundation for the colony's infrastructure. This innovative approach minimized reliance on Earth imports and maximized resource utilization, a crucial aspect of sustainable colonization efforts.

The construction process was meticulous yet efficient. The printer module carefully layered the Martian-derived cement between prefabricated walls, ensuring robust protection against the harsh radiation prevalent on the Martian surface.

In addition to the structural elements, the module incorporated essential amenities into the buildings. Airlocks, windows offering glimpses of the Martian landscape, occlus for natural light, rover robots for exploration, atmospheric control systems for habitability, and basic necessities like toilets and sinks were seamlessly integrated into the colony's architecture.

Each of the crew buildings was designed to comfortably accommodate up to ten members. The interior layout was thoughtfully planned. There are private sleeping quarters on the lower levels. A communal social area on the second floor fosters camaraderie and relaxation. The bath and shower facilities were placed on the third floor, improving privacy. The second floor doubled as a functional workspace equipped with all the necessary tools and equipment to support the team's research endeavors on Mars.

Ares Haven Colony stands as a beacon of human achievement in the Martian wilderness, blending cutting-edge technology with resourcefulness and sustainability to establish a foothold for humanity on the Red Planet.

We landed without incident. Our shuttle had the same features as the Moon's shuttle, which we named the

Archimedes. It could perform vertical landings and takeoffs, enabling the craft to land almost anywhere.

The lead scientist, Niels Heisenberg, met us at the landing site and walked directly to Buzz, speaking with a great deal of animation.

My first thought was, "Does the colony have a critical issue?" Niels finished speaking. Buzz nodded. Niels pointed to the colony's entryway and escorted us inside. Once inside, we removed our headgear.

Buzz looked to the team and said, "There has been a distress call sent by a supply ship heading for this location. Ten days from Mars, the ship's propulsion system failed. They are adrift in the starkness of space."

"God Speed is the closest craft in the area. We will not be spending time on the colony. I have given Niel the programs outlining deuterium and Helium-3 conversion performed on Luna Colony. Theo will remain on site to assist."

"The Helium-3 collection and the follow-on fusion with deuterium process are critical for Ares Haven's sustainability. The colony is frequently inundated with sandstorms, causing challenges in maintaining power collection from the solar panels. It is a constant battle keeping them clean."

I voiced my concerns aloud, "This will cause us to lose twenty-plus days, deviating from our mission, searching for the God Particle. Ten days to the ship's last location, an unknown number of days to assist in repairs, and ten-plus days just to get us back this far."

Buzz turned to me and, with a stern visage, said, "We are the closest; people come first."

Realizing he was right, I grumbled, "ok."

We said goodbye to Theo, donned our headgear, and left for Archimedes, back into the bleak Martian atmosphere.

Buzz sat in his pilot seat, took a deep breath, and called to Angelica, our onboard computer, "Angelica, take us home." A soft, melodic voice responded, "Yes, sir, homeward bound."

Archimedes, our trusty transport, lifted off vertically, then smoothly rotated its thrusters ninety degrees. In the blink of an eye, we were pressed back into our seats, leaving the colony far behind.

Disembarking Archimedes, we quickly had a brisk planning session. After the briefing, Juan swiftly returned to his workstation to search for the disabled craft. With precision, he located the ship's last known position and meticulously plotted an intercept course.

I reminded the team that the asteroid Psyche is still heading our way, and we should not squander the opportunity to collect data from it. Buzz agreed and asked for options to achieve both of these goals.

Gene stood, smiling confidently as she looked around the room. "We *can* do both," she said, pacing slightly. "Hermes can launch toward Psyche now, land, collect the data and samples, and rendezvous with us during our return to Mars."

She glanced at Juan, who nodded. "Based on my calculations," she continued, "and Juan's confirmation, it'll take ten days to reach the Bounty, five for repairs. If it is too damaged, we will have to rig a tow, and then get back to Mars."

I leaned forward, skeptical. "That's assuming everything goes perfectly. No delays, no system faults. What if Hermes fails to land or transmit data? We're splitting our focus right when we should be unified."

Gene didn't flinch. "Hermes is fully autonomous. The mission parameters are already programmed. And it only needs six days to intercept Psyche. That gives us a wide enough window. Even if there's a hiccup, we're still within operational margins."

Vector crossed his arms, his expression doubtful. "You're assuming the asteroid's surface is stable enough for a soft landing. We haven't seen real-time data on the terrain."

"I accounted for that," Gene replied coolly. "The latest projection models from Theo's instruments show a stable rotation and consistent reflectivity. If the terrain changes drastically, Hermes' AI will abort and continue mapping from orbit. It's not a blind dive."

Captain Albright raised a hand to quiet the room. "So, you're saying, Gene, that Hermes launches now, reaches Psyche in six days, completes its mission independently, and we rendezvous with it on our return from the Bounty?"

"That's right, sir," she confirmed.

I sighed. "It's tight. Real tight."

Vector muttered, "And risky."

"But not reckless," Gene said firmly. "It's calculated risk. We get both missions done—no compromise to the rescue, no loss of scientific opportunity.   We may find needed minerals for Mar's fusion power plant."

A pause settled over the room.

Captain Albright nodded slowly. "You've made your case, Gene. It's bold. But bold is what we signed up for."

He looked around the table. "Any strong objections?"

Vector exhaled through his nose but shook his head. "Just don't expect me to say 'I told you so' quietly if something goes sideways."

I smirked. "We'll put it in the mission log in all caps."

The room chuckled, tension easing slightly.

I raised my voice slightly. "Let's keep our eyes on the primary objective—*the God Particle*. Everything else is secondary."

There were murmurs of agreement. The decision was made.

As we filed out of the briefing room, Buzz's voice cut through the hum of movement.

"Alright, everyone, focus. We need to know everything about the *Bounty* before we reach her."

The air crackled with anticipation. No one lingered; each team member practically jogged to their stations, eager to immerse themselves in the *Bounty's* propulsion data. Screens flickered to life, filling the room with a glow of cascading diagnostics and simulations.

Juan moved with practiced precision to the Hermes control console. He pulled up the asteroid's last recorded telemetry, fingers flying across the keys. Within moments, he had charted an intercept with Psyche, a clean and efficient trajectory projected in luminous arcs across the display.

Within thirty minutes, Hermes launched toward Psyche.

Seated at his console, Juan turned to the team with a sheepish grin. "Okay, I messed up. Hermes will intercept Psyche in four days, not six."

Buzz strolled over, clapped a hand on Juan's shoulder, and smirked. "Four days, huh? What happened—your calculator ran out of batteries, or did you start counting Martian days again?"

Laughter rippled through the room.

Juan held up his hands in mock surrender. "Fine, fine. Next time I'll use an abacus

The room erupted again as Juan chuckled, shaking his head and turning back to his console.

We were on our way to aid the distressed craft Bounty. Hermes had its course set, hurtling toward Psyche, and both missions began.

The day stretched on, with hours blending into one another as we delved into the intricacies of our plans to assist Bounty. We explored various contingencies, speculating on the nature of the impending challenge and brainstorming the most effective strategies for swift resolution.

The contingencies we discussed ranged from the likely to the extreme. At the forefront was the possibility that *Bounty*'s propulsion system had suffered a cascading electrical failure. If so, Juan and Vector had prepared a modular repair package that could be installed with minimal manual interface and guided remotely if needed.

We also considered the worst-case scenario: total loss of life support. Though their transmissions suggested stable internal conditions, we couldn't risk assuming continuity. Gene ran emergency response simulations, ensuring our medical bay could stabilize and treat up to six incoming patients, including those with hypoxia or radiation exposure.

Gene flagged a concern about orbital drift. If *Bounty* had lost fine thruster control, it could slip from its holding pattern and destabilize. Buzz proposed a controlled intercept using our maneuvering jets and tethering options to hold *Bounty* in a safe orientation. We also prepped an auto-docking override. Manual docking had its risks, but in a pinch, Juan said he could pilot blindfolded.

Communication blackouts were another variable. Gene suggested a relay workaround using our satellite array to piggyback messages if *Bounty*'s antenna had been damaged. It was a low-latency fix, but better than silence.

Each plan had branches. We diagrammed them, discussed hand signals for zero-comm operations, and ran drills in half-gravity—tedious, tiring, necessary. By the time we stopped, we had an answer for almost every plausible scenario, and a few implausible ones, too.

As the day unwound, we slowly migrated to our racks for rest.

This has been a long day. I was so looking forward to touring Ares Haven. Well, duty called us with a higher priority. After resolving this incident, I hope we can focus on our priority, the God Particle, soon.

DUEL OPERATIONS

March 9th, 2036

This morning began with Gene's excited announcement over the internal communication system: "Hermes has located the asteroid Psyche; tomorrow it will be in position to land on the equator."

Since its launch, *Hermes* had collected data on Psyche during its approach to the intercept point. Equipped with a spectrometer and thermal inertia instruments, Gene was able to determine the asteroid's size, shape, and probable mineral composition prior to landing.

Psyche had an irregular, potato-like shape, measuring approximately thirty miles in length and forty miles in width.

Gene used the data collected by Hermes to generate a 3D rendering of Psyche, revealing small craters scattered across its surface. Based on the scans, she determined that Psyche was composed of a mixture of rock, metal, and frozen water beneath its crust.

Further analysis revealed the presence of potential pockets of Helium-3 and deuterium below the surface—both essential elements for sustaining Mars' fusion power plant. This discovery was thrilling, as it addressed a major concern regarding the long-term feasibility of fusion energy on Mars.

Mars has the same problem as Earth, a limited supply of Helium-3. Without a steady supply it will be difficult to sustain a fusion power plant. Finding these resources could be a game-changer for fusion energy on Ares Colony.

Theo and the Ares Haven team knew the challenge but refused to fail. This discovery may help Ares have sufficient resources to power the fusion plant for many decades. Of course, this will depend on the amount of Helium-3 and deuterium extracted from Psyche.

Sitting at the briefing table, sipping coffee and tea, we listened as Gene briefed us on the next phase of our mission: getting Hermes landed and collecting additional data and minerals. Hermes was set to land tomorrow.

Juan had meticulously prepared the landing vectors. Gene provided a mineral collection schedule and, most importantly, the timing for drilling through the crater's surface in search of Helium-3 and deuterium.

Gene's information had energized Vector, who now fully immersed himself in the plans. With his thick German accent and unmistakable enthusiasm, Vector stood up and declared, "First, we must determine the quantity of Helium-3 and deuterium available. Once we have that data, I will transmit Psyche's coordinates to Theo. He will coordinate with Ares Haven to develop an intercept course for the ships to reach Psyche and to collect as much material as possible."

Buzz, with his calming demeanor, put things into perspective. "Stay focused on our primary mission to rendezvous with the Bounty and resolve its issues. Once accomplished, we will set our course towards Mars, collect Hermes, and continue our quest to find the God Particle. Juan proceeds with Hermes' landing on Psyche.

The remainder of the day fell into our routine. Juan monitored the ship, conducting maintenance to ensure computers and engines were functioning at their optimum.

Buzz reviewed the course navigation date, determining God Speed's progress toward Bounty.

Gene, Vector, and I conducted long-range surveys focused on deep space phenomena, specifically the Interstellar Medium. We studied its composition, density, and magnetic fields in the regions between stars.

After reviewing the day's events, I am satisfied with the decision to deviate from our course to the Heliosphere for the greater good.

It goes without saying that we must take on both of these objectives. We can possibly save lives, and a colony will have sustainable power, paving the way for civilization to grow on Mars.

Questions float in my head: Will there be more distractions? What might they be? Will we ever reach the heliosphere to begin our search?

Well, at least with the Hermes landing tomorrow, the team will be fully engaged as we trudge toward the Bounty and her challenges. I am excited to see what we will learn from Hermes.

After dinner and one drink, I settled down to read C. S. Lewis's "Screwtape Letters." It was a great distraction from my everyday science endeavors. It made me wonder if there are angels and demons. Maybe the God Particle will provide some enlightenment.

I close by expressing my appreciation for all team members' health, good spirits, and readiness to take on whatever comes next. Tomorrow's Hermes landing on Psyche will be exciting.

As H. G. Wells once said, "What on earth would a man do with himself if something did not stand in his way?" — H.G. Wells (*June 1940*)

WHISPERS FROM PSYCHE

March 10th, 2036

Lying in my rack, half asleep, I suddenly remembered that today Hermes would be landing on Psyche. I leapt up, rushed through the unsatisfying sonic shower, dressed quickly, and dashed into the control room to check the landing status.

Entering the control room, I saw everyone huddled around Gene's control panel, as she reviewed data transmitted from Hermes. For a moment, they all turned and looked in my direction. I was late!

Buzz chuckled, "Did you plan on missing this adventure?"

I sheepishly smiled and walked briskly to where the team stood behind Gene. I mumbled a question, "Did I miss anything? No response.

There were three monitors on the console. One to Gene's left displayed radioactive emission data. A second in the center, displayed telemetry transmitted from Hermes. The monitor to her right showed a ship symbol indicating Hermes' current position relative to Psyche.

Technology never ceases to amaze me. Tens of thousands of miles away, we could see Hermes slowly closing in on the asteroid. A dark mass, potato-shaped, appeared to have red and blue lines on the surface.

Gene reported, "Psyche measures 157km X 30km. The colors on the surface could indicate different mineral deposits. There is a massive crater in the center. That is where I planned for Hermes to land and collect samples."

Turning to her left to check the radioactive readings, Gene screamed, "Holy crap! It looks like Helium-3 and deuterium deposits are within the crater. Let's not get too excited until Hermes lands and begins drilling to extract samples."

Gene turned to Juan to her left and said, "Are you ready?"

Juan smiled. Grabbed the control stick and began slowly guiding Hermes onto the crater.

A perfect landing. Hermes landed exactly at the coordinates Gene had provided; directly over what had been identified as Helium-3 and deuterium deposits.

Juan smiled with pride on the successful landing. He laughed, saying, 'Now let's see what the robot Rover can do.'

Juan typed in a set of Instructions directing Rover to come alive, exit Hermes and begin collecting samples.

Specifically, surface minerals and frozen water deposits. Once accomplished, it will return to Hermes.

Suddenly, without warning, Hermes autonomously lit up its engines as if to launch back to God Speed.

As Hermes began leaving the surface, the rover had traversed halfway down the exit ramp and stopped, struggling to maintain an upright position. Seconds later, it lost the battle and fell ten feet to the surface.

In an effort to regain control of Hermes, Juan sat at his console frantically keying over ride commands. Hermes did not respond.

Buzz yelled, "Just shut down the engines!"

"Are you nuts?" Juan screamed, sneering. "Hermes may hit the surface, causing unacceptable damage."

Hermes fought Juan for control. With a herculean effort, he kept the ship hovering in place.

Neither Hermes nor Juan had complete control. The ship maintained a stationary distance from the surface—a stalemate. In a last-ditch effort, Juan sent a "kill" command that disabled Hermes's autonomous controls. A green light flashed on Juan's console, confirming he had manual control.

Gripping the control stick tightly, Juan tested Hermes' response. He softly said, "I have complete control." Then, he gently set the craft down on the crater.

With an audible sigh from all, the tension subsided. Until I thought about Rover. In a frantic voice, I ask, "Where is Rover? Did it survive the fall?

Juan looked at Gene, who had already taken control of Hermes' cameras. She began rotating them, scanning the terrain for the rover.
Silence filled the room. Gene switched from one camera feed to another, rotating each one methodically as she searched for the rover.

After an intense ten minutes, Gene smiled, pointed at the monitor, and, with relief in her voice, said, "There it is. Hah! She survived the fall. Rover is collecting samples."

Flipping a switch on the console, Gene ran a quick internal diagnostics. She spoke, saying, "With the exception of a few dents, all is well with Rover."

Satisfied with Rover's status, Juan turned to the team and said, "To ensure Hermes will be able to regain autonomous control, I need to send reboot instructions. This should resolve the anomaly. The reboot will take two hours to complete. During this period, we won't be able to communicate with Hermes or track Rover."

The two hours passed quickly. The reboot was successful. We communicated with Rover, and the onboard cameras gave us a bird's-eye view of its progress.

Rover took three additional hours to complete its assigned collection instructions and returned to Hermes.

After docking with Hermes, it began transmitting a plethora of data it had collected. Rover identified metals and minerals. Among the data, the most exciting find was the location of Helium-3 and deuterium in the center of the crater.

In anticipation of the next evolution, we congregated behind Gene as she instructed Hermes to drill and insert a sensor into the surface. The sensor collected data identifying the location and estimated volume of Helium-3 and deuterium available for extraction.

We stared at the console as the data flowed in. Gene excitedly turned to Juan and said, "Look at these numbers; there is a large deposit of Helium-3 within the asteroid. It encompasses one square mile below the crater's surface. Undoubtedly sufficient to support the Mars colony."

"There appears to be deuterium just beyond the Helium-3 deposits. She jumped up and smacked me on the shoulder, saying, "This is better than when gold was discovered in America."

Buzz stood between Gene and Juan. Placing his hand

on their shoulders, said, "Outstanding job. Consolidate the data. Once ready, I will send it to Theo at Ares Haven."

Three hours later, Buzz transmitted the data and Psyche's coordinates to Theo on Ares Haven. He recommended loading the Helium-3 and deuterium extraction equipment and tankers onto their transport ships and set a course for Psyche ASAP.

Meanwhile, Juan issued commands to Hermes, instructing it to launch and head for Ares Haven. Once we return to Mars, Hermes will be retrieved.

The remainder of the day was uneventful. The team gathered in the galley for dinner and discussed the day's events.

Buzz was the last to enter the galley. Holding a small box under his arm, he said, "Outstanding job today, all. To celebrate this success, I have something for everyone."

He pulled the box from under his arm. Opening the box, it revealed fine Cuban cigars. We each took one in turn and lit them up. A sense of satisfaction could be felt throughout the room, and the aroma of fine cigars filled the air.

Sitting here in my berthing area, I am having two whiskeys tonight. It will take that for me to unwind. This is why I do science. Excitement and wonder are abundant if one only looks.

Here's hoping we are as successful in aiding the Bounty. I do tire of waiting to get on with our primary mission, God Particle.

TO THE BOUNTY

March 14th, 2036

I woke up quickly, went to the galley, grabbed a cup of coffee, and headed for the briefing room. Our primary mission was the Bounty.

As usual, I was the last to get to the briefing.

Juan informed the team, "Last night, before I went to bed, I was able to communicate with the Bounty."

"We should be on station to assist them by midday."

"The ship has been using its thrusters to maintain position, Captain Blight said his team is in good spirits, though they're anxious to get underway and resume their journey to Mars."

"After being disabled for so long, their nerves are understandably frayed. Their biggest complaint?" Juan paused with a smile. "They're down to their last pot of coffee."

Laughter rippled through the room. Everyone nodded smiling. Coffee is sacred out here.

"Unfortunately, the ship's engineer sustained second-degree burns on her hands while attempting to shut down the propulsion system and prevent a catastrophic failure. Captain Blight confirmed her injuries have been treated, and no additional medical support is needed."

94

Once Juan had completed his brief, Buzz stood and said, "Okay, let's get the people taken care of. Juan, get to your console, reach out to Bounty, and see what other information you can gather. We will meet back here in one hour to solidify a plan."

Juan left heading from the control room.

Entering the control room, Juan could be heard communicating with the Bounty, collecting additional information about its condition.

One hour later, Juan returned to the briefing room. The team had gathered. He reported, "We are approximately 100 yards from the Bounty. Captain Blight informed me that no one had re-entered the engine room since the accident. He is not sure what we may encounter when we move in to assess the damage. Buzz, I recommend we don our hazmat gear before we ingress into the engineering."

Buzz replied, "That's a good idea. Give the gear a once-over to be sure it's ready."

The team sat around the conference table, savoring their coffee as the aroma filled the room. The conversation focused on devising strategies to aid the Bounty. Each one brought their unique perspective and expertise to the table.

Strolling toward the bridge, I peered out and caught sight of the Bounty, a mere one hundred yards ahead. The vessel boasted a modern design, its sleek form gliding effortlessly through the void. Its retractable wings, reminiscent of advanced long-distance supply ships, were folded in, giving it a streamlined appearance.

Buzz called me back to the conference room. As I approached, I could see the seriousness etched into his face. He gestured for me to take a seat before outlining the plan.

"Alright, here's the situation," Buzz began, his tone grave but focused. "According to the Bounty's damage report, their primary drive seal conduit is shot. Juan will take the shuttle over to begin repairs, but he'll need backup. That's where we come in."

He paused for a moment, then continued. "We'll monitor all of the Bounty's onboard systems while the work is underway. I don't know what kind of shape their crew is in. Being stranded in space takes a toll. They may not be at their best. Juan's safety is our top priority."

I nodded, already mentally preparing myself for the task ahead. Repairing a primary drive was no small feat, but with Buzz leading the way, I felt confident we could tackle the challenge.

Juan had the technical know-how, but it would be delicate work. Buzz continued, his gaze meeting mine with a sense of urgency. "We need to ensure everything goes smoothly, or else the Bounty will need a tow. This will delay our mission searching for The God Particle."

I leaned in, absorbing every detail Buzz was laying out. "The success of this mission depends on our ability to work together seamlessly and execute the repairs flawlessly.

We have the spare parts, the proper skills," Buzz declared, his voice firm and resolute. He continued, "Let's get to work and get that ship back up and running."

With a shared nod of determination, we rose from the table, ready to face whatever challenges lay ahead. The fate of the Bounty rested in our hands, and failure was not an option.

I was assigned to visually monitor the Bounty, looking for unusual gas venting or leaks. Buzz, a seasoned pilot, would be at his pilot's console prepared to execute tactical maneuvers, if necessary. He would be in continuous communication with Juan.

Vector had analyzed the Bounty's propulsion system schematics and created suggested solutions for repairing the damage. These were loaded into his suits' heads-up display and available to Juan when he got on board."

Gene, who holds a PhD in medicine, would be on standby to assist the Bounty's crew with any medical emergencies. She also manned the long-distance sensors, looking for any space debris or anomalies that could collide with the Bounty or us.

Around midday, we had closed within ten yards of Bounty. I watched the Archimedes (our shuttle) gracefully close the final distance and dock. Juan radioed, "Archimedes docked. I am heading into Bounty. I will advise when on-site in engineering."

Entering the Bounty, Juan was met by Captain Blight. With a haggard look of exhaustion, Blight said, "Thank you. We have been out here for three weeks. Our food supplies are running low. We thought we might die before our distress call was heard and help arrived. Did you bring some coffee?"

Both men laughed. Juan reached into his backpack pulled out several packets of coffee grounds. Smiling said, "Will this do."

Juan smiled, placed a hand on the pilot's shoulder, and said, "How about taking me to the engine room? We believe we know your problem, and I have brought the parts to get you up and running."

Blight pointed to his left, saying, "This way."

Walking past the crew's galley, Juan saw the other crew members sitting drinking the last of their coffee. He stuck his head in and said, "Hi. We should have your engine back online in a few hours, and you can get on your way."

Captain Blight, threw the coffee supplies on to the closet table. He said, "Now we do not have to drink one-half ration coffee." The crew erupted with a great cheer.

The engineer raised her bandaged burned hands and with a painful look, said, "I would help, but as you can see, I would be not of any use."

Entering engineering, Juan began his analysis.

After twenty minutes, He radioed, "Buzz, I've examined the drive and have everything needed to get this ship operational within the hour."

"However, I found a critical design flaw. The bolts in the drive conduit were manufactured with substandard material, leading to fractures in the threading. When the drive engaged, the vibrations caused the bolts to break free. Two bolts became wedged into the seal, causing a tear."

"Once the seal was compromised, it was only a matter of time before the drive failed. They are lucky that the propulsion drive did not explode."

"This same issue occurred on the shuttle Aster with catastrophic results. The Aster's drive released fuel into the main cabin, igniting. When rescue ships arrived, they found only debris and one survivor who had been in her exo-suit preparing to do a spacewalk at the time of the explosion."

Buzz responded, "Excellent work. Ensure you assist the Bounty's engineer in drafting additional routine maintenance checks on the system."

After completing the repairs, Juan returned to the shuttle and said goodbye.

Just before the outer hatch was secured, the Bounty's captain could be heard shouting, "Wait." Juan watched the captain running toward him carrying a box. He stopped, smiling, and said, "This is the best we could do to thank you and God Speed's crew for the assist. I hope it is enough." He shook Juan's hand, turned, and was gone.

Juan turned and closed the hatch with the usual metallic click, confirming a secure seal.

With a smile of gratitude, he placed the box in a secure location.

Strapping himself into the pilot's seat, undocked from the Bounty and set a course for God Speed.

Juan returned, satisfied with his work. After cleaning up and enjoying a hearty meal, he sat at his computer and compiled a mishap report for the next two hours. Once completed, the report was transmitted to the leadership at both Ares Haven and Luna Colony. He included several recommendations, the most important of which was to conduct a complete inspection of their shuttle craft. Each colony operated two ships of the same class as the *Bounty*.

During the evening debriefing on the day's events, Juan suddenly sprang up and dashed out of the room, exclaiming, "Man, I forgot something in the shuttle!" Moments later, he returned with a broad smile, holding a nondescript box.

"In appreciation for the assist, the Bounty's captain sent over this thank-you gift," he announced as he placed the box on the table.

Curiosity buzzed as we speculated about the contents. Buzz, ever the enthusiastic one, stood up, brandished his knife, and carefully pried open the box.

An audible OOOH escaped from Juan and Buzz as the lid came off. Buzz looked up, with a Cheshire cat grin spreading across his face, and triumphantly held up a bottle of single malt whiskey.

The room erupted in cheers. "A case of single malt whiskey!" I shouted. "Cigars and whiskey for a nightcap!"

After the debriefing and dinner concluded, we retired to the galley for cigars and the exquisite whiskey. It was the perfect reward for our hard work. As the evening drew to a close, I felt a profound warmth and contentment, more than I have in some time.

Looking out my port window, I could see the Bounty gliding next to us as we both made our way to Mars.

I savor the sense of accomplishment and camaraderie that made this moment truly special.

Sleep would come quickly tonight.

RETURN TO MARS

March 24th, 2036

The ten-day transit back to Mars was uneventful. Arriving early today, I expected we would be able to visit the colony before getting back on course.

We escorted the Bounty, ensuring a safe transit to Mars. Along the way, we swapped crews, allowing each member to receive training and experience in a different craft.   One never knows when additional education may come in handy.

On the sixth day, both crews were stuck in the doldrums. During breakfast, Juan suddenly jumped up with great excitement, startling everyone. He began chattering rapidly, "Let's have some fun. We should select a crew member from each ship for a competition."

Silence filled the room, and excitement began to rumble throughout the galley as we blurted out ideas.

Juan held up his hand, with a twinkle in his eye, chuckled, saying, "The competition should be something physical like a race."

He looked around at the others, grinning. "Our ships aren't big enough for anything indoors. So how about this: one crew member from each team suits up in an exo-suit and races from one ship to the other."

Murmurs of interest rose.

"We'll position the ships three hundred yards apart," he continued. "The main forward thruster can only be used once at the start. After that, just short stabilizing bursts to stay on course. No second chances."

He paused for effect, then added with a mischievous smile, "Losing team serves dinner and drinks for two days."

Racing out of the galley, we gathered in the control room as Buzz excitedly flipped the radio transmission switch, saying, "Bounty, this is Buzz from God Speed. Request to speak to Captain Blight."

For a few moments, the radio crackled, and silence filled the control room, waiting for a response.

Finally, the radio crackled to life.

"This is Captain Blight. Buzz, what can I do for you?"

Buzz replied, "Captain, this morning at breakfast, the crew complained about how bored they've become. A conversation started, tossing around suggestions for some relief. The unanimous choice? A competition with the Bounty."

Blight's response was drowned out by a sudden uproar of cheering and shouting from his crew in the background. He laughed and called out, "Calm down, everyone!" Then, pressing the transmission key again, he said excitedly, "What do you have in mind?"

"We propose one crew member from each ship dons an exo-suit and races three hundred yards—from one ship to the other," Buzz suggested.

A chorus of cheers erupted again through the radio. Blight responded, barely containing his own laughter, "Roger that. Godspeed! We accept the challenge."

Buzz replied, "Juan has volunteered to represent us. We will meet at 1400 hours, with God Speed being the starting point. We will race to Bounty 300 yards away."

Everyone in the control room smiled, slapping each other on the back. Buzz shouted over the cacophony, "Let's get ready!"

At 1400 hours, the two competitors suited up and stood next to our exit hatch, buzzing with excitement.

The ships were holding stations three hundred yards apart. Crew members from both ships peered from every available port to watch the race.

The radios buzzed with excited voices cheering on their team member.

Juan was heard saying to Paula, the Bounty's racer, "When you lose, I expect you'll be serving me steak tonight." They both laughed.

Buzz picked up the microphone and clicked it twice, indicating silence on the line.

Enthusiastically, he announced, "Okay, competitors, disembark the ship, grab the external handholds, and wait for my signal to launch. Remember the rules.

Juan and Paula exited the ship.

Juan closed the hatch. A sucking sound could be heard, confirming a sealed hatch.

They both held onto the hatch handhold. Buzz asked, "Are the competitors ready?"

Simultaneously, both shouted, "Yes!"

Buzz, laughing almost uncontrollably, burst out, "Go!"

Juan and Paula pushed off the ship at the same time.

Using the momentum from their push, neither activated their forward thruster, knowing it would only work once and had to be timed just right. They drifted in silence, slowly coasting toward the Bounty.

Halfway there, their momentum dwindled until they were practically stationary, adrift between the two ships.

Juan turned in place, performing a slow 360-degree roll. He looked over to Paula and laughed.

"Well," he called, "should we take our only shot and see who gets there first?"

Paula smirked. "Or," she teased, "do you want to drive these guys crazy and just float here for a while?"

Juan laughed. "Tempting. But nope. Let's count down and hit it together."

Paula nodded.

"Three, two, one."

They fired their thrusters at the same time, shooting forward in a clean line toward the Bounty. The crews from both ships watched in tense silence.

Ten minutes later, they were within feet of the finish. Juan's voice came through softly on comms, "Paula... let's make it a tie."

She glanced at him, then nodded.

Together, they reached out and touched the Bounty at the same instant.

Disappointed groans and boos erupted from both crews. There would be no victory celebration and no serving dinner for either side.

Just laughter from Juan and Paula, floating there, smug and satisfied.

After the race, our team settled into the task at hand.

Around 1400 today, Ares Haven radioed, "God Speed. This is Ares Control. Be advised that we are launching a convoy headed for Psyche."

In awe, we watched as the convoy emerged from the dark silhouette of the colony: three massive ore haulers, each flanked by a pair of nimble escort craft, and two fuel tankers bringing the lifeblood for the mining operations to come. Automated cargo drones clung to the hulls like barnacles, ready to detach and begin shuttling supplies the moment they arrived.

One by one, their engines flared, forming bright spears of light against the black, marking the beginning of their long journey to the asteroid. In a flash, the entire convey disappeared into the blackness of space.

It was more than just a launch. It was a testament to months of preparation. Our God Speed team had played a key role in locating the elements that now justified this mission. Pride swelled within us, knowing we had made a tangible difference in the future of the Ares Haven Colony.

Theo reported that Ares Haven's teams would be able to successfully extract enough Helium-3 and deuterium to power the fusion plant for ten years. This estimate doesn't account for the Helium-3 available on Mars' surface.

With this success, Ares Haven is much closer to establishing permanent communities on Mars.

We spent a few hours on Mars's surface, receiving a quick tour of the facilities. The highlight was the newly minted fusion power plant, which provides the primary power to Ares Haven. This is a significant upgrade from the previous solar power cells.

The constant presence of Mars's red sand severely hampers solar cells' efficiency, which could reduce their energy collection to around 50% at best.

The dim yellow lighting generated by the solar cells has been replaced by bright white LED lighting, a much-appreciated improvement.

Late into the evening, the Mars team rewarded us with a banquet, including fine whiskey and cigars—a small token of appreciation for our part in finding Helium-3 on Psyche.

After dinner, we loaded on the shuttle for transit back to God Speed.

Hermes had already returned to the ship in preparation for our departure from Mars orbit.

While in transit to God Speed, Buzz informed us, "Rest tonight, for tomorrow we get back on track, getting underway for the Heliosphere to find the God Particle."

Looking around the ship, renewed excitement and anticipation could be seen on everyone's face.

We have been traveling for more than three hundred days, knowing that years of travel are required before we reach our destination. I wonder if this enthusiasm will burn out.

Arriving onboard God Speed, the team gathered to discuss our departure and identify key way points for additional scientific exploration.

Buzz stood and began, "Space Command has a few requests for us to accomplish along the way, provided it doesn't significantly impact our primary mission."

Gene interrupted Buzz, asking, "I thought our goal was the God Particle and nothing else?"

Buzz responded thoughtfully, "Well, we could spend the next few years doing nothing until we reach the Heliosphere, or we could conduct possible groundbreaking science. "Look what we have experienced since we departed from Earth. We will be reaching parts of our solar system never explored by humans."

Considering Buzz's comments, Gene tilted her head and nodded, saying, "Well, I hadn't considered that."

Buzz continued, "Our first mission is Jupiter's moon, Europa. We have data and images from the research ship Europa Clipper, launched in 2024."

"Its mission was to orbit Europa and collect data enabling scientists to determine the best location for future missions to land safely."

"Europa's environment is often regarded as Earth-like within our solar system. It is a prime candidate for exploring the potential for sustaining human life beyond our planet."

"This moon of Jupiter's is believed to harbor a vast subsurface ocean beneath its icy crust. Possibly containing the essential ingredients for life."

Buzz continued, "Before arriving at Europa, our task is to communicate with Europa Clipper, extract all available data, and analyze it before sending Hermes to land and collect water and mineral samples."

"The data will enable us to select the best landing site for Hermes."

"Hermes data collection should provide sufficient information for Space Command to determine the sustainability of life on Europa."

This mission was not a foregone conclusion. Buzz needed a unanimous agreement from the team. Without consensus, we would simply fly by Jupiter and its moons without stopping.

Buzz looked to the team, "Take a day to consider whether there is value in moving on this mission. I will take your input at tomorrow's briefing."

"Each member must weigh the benefits of contributing to scientific knowledge against the time devoted to the God Particle mission."

With the meeting finished, we went our separate ways to consider these options.

Looking out into the vast emptiness of space, I am in awe of how dark and bleak the abyss is.

One can see stars and planets, but they are minuscule relative to the blackness. This causes me to pause and wonder why anyone would want to do this.

In my case, I am trying to fill the void within myself left by the loss of my daughter. Hope springs eternal; maybe the God Particle does exist.

Turning my thoughts to tomorrow's mission decision, I am perplexed. Since we will pass by Europa en route to our destination, what harm would it be to collect data? We are the first humans to travel this far into space.

This is an opportunity to collect data that may help Space Command determine whether human life is viable on

Europa.

On the other hand, what if something goes wrong and we cannot continue on our primary mission? Well, the what-ifs are out of my control.

I plan to recommend landing Hermes on Europa, collect the data, and send Hermes with the data and samples to Ares Haven for further analysis.

Ares Haven is better equipped to isolate the samples and perform quality analysis. The colony will send Space Command its findings and recommendations.

This does not preclude us from analyzing the data Hermes collects in "real-time." We have programmed Hermes to transmit data as it is being collected and stored in its database.

This will be settled at our briefing tomorrow. For now, I am ready for a good night's sleep.

NEW ADVENTURE - EUROPA

March 25th, 2036

In the early hours, the team stirred with a quiet but palpable anticipation, every thought focused on the looming decision about the Europa mission.

Gathering in the galley, seated around the table, we savored eggs, sausage, toast, and coffee, the clinking of utensils punctuating the lively chatter. Speculation danced through the air like tendrils of steam, swirling around the room as we mulled over the implications of our next move. Are we going to take on the Europa mission?

Eventually, we migrated to the briefing room. Buzz and Juan were deep in discussion about God Speed's performance. Juan reported that all engines were running at peak efficiency, and their recent maintenance kept the ship in top condition.

Buzz asked, "If we take on this mission to Europa, will it put undue stress on *God Speed* and risk our God Particle mission?"

Looking him straight in the eye, Juan confidently replied, "Sir, she can handle this and much more."

Buzz's faint smile betrayed his satisfaction with the answer.

Vector arrived late, grumbling about the early wake-up call required for breakfast before the meeting. His disgruntled demeanor added a touch of realism to the scene, a reminder of the mundane challenges inherent in space exploration.

Buzz stood, cleared his throat, and said, "I hold in my hand an assignment request from Space Command that I will read. Once finished, the floor will be opened for discussion. Know that this is not an order, but a request from Space Command."

He began reading, "Captain, this mission request is for your team to land a probe on Europa. The goal will be to collect minerals, water samples, and additional environmental data in an effort to determine the viability of establishing a colony on its surface."

"Accepting this mission is a decision for you and your team to proceed. We realize this may delay your reaching the Heliosphere, but we feel it is necessary to support human existence."

"Considering the current state of the Human Race, wars, plagues, and environmental disasters, it is imperative to find another habitable planet. Without an alternative, Human consciousness may be lost."

Silence filled the room as we contemplated this information. To many of us, the prospect of this additional mission's enormity loomed heavily.

The possibility of discovering transformational scientific information impacting a decision to place a colony on Europa must be weighed against the time lost deviating from the primary mission, God Particle.

Looking around the room, Buzz saw our concern. He said, "I believe the Europa mission poses minimal risk to our primary mission, the God Particle. The plan is to launch Hermes, land her on Europa, and be on our way. When Hermes has completed her mission, Juan will send instructions for Hermes to transit to Ares Haven."

Buzz continued, "After all, what else would occupy our time during the remaining years of our journey to the Heliosphere?"

As Buzz sought our input and votes, the gravity of the decision weighed heavily on each of us. It was a pivotal moment that would shape the course of our mission and, perhaps, the future of space exploration itself.

Vector, Gene, and I voted to seize the opportunity and conduct this research. As scientists, we were born to collect data, analyze it, and make informed decisions.

Theo had one concern: losing Hermes. He worried it might be needed later during our voyage.

Instead of sending Hermes to Mars, Theo proposed bringing the samples onboard for analysis.

Theo said, "We have years to go to reach our goal. Why not take this opportunity to be the scientist whose findings support Europa's viability to sustain life?"

"Hermes will collect ice, potential water, and other minerals. We're right here; we should gain the recognition. Other than that, I'm on board."

Buzz responded, "Theo, Hermes' value lies in landing on the surface of the surface, deploying its robot, and collecting data to determine the viability of life on a planet or moon."

"After Europa, we have no real use for it. Besides, Ares Haven is better equipped to perform in-depth sample analysis. Remember, we still have the shuttle for transiting if necessary."

Frowning with dissatisfaction, Theo nodded, affirming his support for the mission. Then, smiling, he said, "Let's do it."

The plan developed quickly. One day before reaching Europa, Juan would program Hermes with landing coordinates and data collection instructions for the mission.

Based on Europa Clipper's data, we selected the equator to be the best location for a landing.

The equator contains ice, metals, and soil that is conducive to drilling.

However, the exact spot has yet to be determined. We have two hundred sixty-one days before reaching Europa. This enables the team sufficient time to analyze Europa Clippers' data more in depth and select the exact landing zone.

The plan was simple yet vital. As Hermes collects samples and readings, it would transmit the data back to our ship in steady streams. Each of us had been assigned specific analysis tasks, tailored to our strengths. These fragments of Europa's secrets would give us purpose and focus, something to ignite our minds during the long, silent years still ahead. Ten more years of travel awaited us before we reached the edge of the Heliosphere. Ten years in which the promise of unraveling the God Particle hovered just beyond our reach. For now, Europa's mysteries would keep us sharp, even as our eyes remained fixed on the far greater discovery that lay ahead.

As the senior scientist, I will coordinate the team's findings, hold brainstorming sessions, and be responsible for the final analysis report.

The rest of the team will review the incoming data. Without the physical samples, our findings will be limited. This will give Space Command advance analysis while they wait for Hermes' transit to Mars. Once Hermes arrives on Ares, the in-depth analysis can begin.

Juan will monitor Hermes' landing and data collection efforts.

Gene is responsible for Hermes' robot, Rover, and its sample collection efforts.

The meeting broke up; excitement oozed from the crew as we headed for our consoles to plan for the landing and data collection.

Tonight, I sit in my berthing, sipping a glass of fine whiskey the Bounty gave us. We have experienced many events since leaving Earth. I could not have foreseen the excitement and opportunities for science we have experienced when volunteering for the God Particle mission. From Luna Colony to Ares Haven, the rescue of the Bounty, finding Helium-3 and deuterium deposits on the asteroid Psyche, and now Hermes landing on Europa, I am left with wonder and anticipation. What lies ahead?

We are still far from the Heliosphere and the God Particle mission. So, I am resigned to one thought: as we delve into the unknown, we must put our fears aside to advance our knowledge.

Is it providence that we have engaged in these adventures, or perhaps an unseen hand is guiding us? Something to consider as I close for tonight.

HERMES ON TO EUROPA

December 11th, 2036

   During our two hundred sixty-one-day transit, the crushing monotony weighed heavily on each member of the crew. The only relief came from immersing ourselves in Europa Clipper's data.

   Hours upon hours of meticulous study, searching for the most promising landing zone for Hermes. Yet even this "distraction" proved more grueling than restful. Selecting an orbital entry point into Europa was no small matter; a single miscalculation could mean disaster on the jagged ice below.

   The debates were relentless, stretching late into the ship's artificial nights. Tempers flared, patience frayed. What began as reasoned discussions soon spiraled into heated confrontations. The sharpest came between Vector and Gene, whose stubborn resolve made compromise nearly impossible. At one point, the two stood nose to nose, fists half-clenched, their voices echoing in the narrow command module.

"Based on my analysis of Europa Clipper," Vector thundered in his thick German accent, "*Thera* is the best area for extracting mineral deposits! The data reflected strong indicators of ice beneath the crust. Ice that could hold the very elements we came to find."

Gene scoffed, sneering, "Vector, you need to review your findings. Your analysis is way off. I spent hours poring over the data. There is no evidence that large quantities of ice or water existed at *Thera*."

"The data supports my findings. *Thrace Maculae* shows significant mineral deposits, large quantities of ice, and possibly water below the surface." With a sardonic laugh, Gene added, "There appears to be Helium-3 deposits beneath *Thrace Maculae's* crust."

Vector's face turned red, he grabbed Gene by the collar, and yelled, "You have no idea what you're talking about!"

Pushing and shoving ensued until Buzz and Juan intervened, reminding them that healthy discourse, not physical violence, was the way of science. The strain of space travel was beginning to wear on Vector, Gene, and possibly all of us. We needed a distraction.

Hopefully, the Hermes launch will provide just that.

Eventually, cooler heads prevailed; we moved forward.

After two hours of debate, the team agreed that Gene's recommendation offered the best chance of success. *Thrace Maculae* was chosen as the landing site.

Situated along Europa's equator, the region contained extensive ice packs ideal for extracting water samples. Data from the Europa Clipper had also highlighted significant concentrations of mineral deposits. In addition, plumes of steam from geysers periodically erupted from the subsurface, providing Hermes with an accessible source of fresh material to analyze. Most intriguing of all, the scans hinted at the presence of Helium-3 deposits. The same possibility Gene had argued for so fiercely during her confrontation with Vector.

We will know more once Hermes begins its mission.

At 10:15 today, Buzz authorized Juan to launch Hermes toward Europa. He estimated orbit entry around 11:00, with the landing effective twenty minutes later.

Standing behind Juan as he controlled Hermes, my eyes were glued to Hermes's external cameras as it approached Europa. My excitement and anxiety were palpable.

Thoughts raced through my mind, trying to grasp the actual weight of our mission. We are not just travelers crossing space; we are pioneers stepping into a realm untouched by humankind. Beyond the edge of every map, into the silence of a frozen moon, we carried the questions of our species. Could the samples hidden beneath Europa's icy crust reveal that microbial life once thrived here, rewriting our understanding of biology itself? Could this thin thread of evidence, fragile yet profound, one day ignite the vision of a human colony beneath its fractured ice plains?

The answers felt close, almost within reach, yet shrouded in the vast uncertainty of the unknown.

It struck me. We are explorers, paving the way for humanity. Magellan and Captain Cook flash across my mind. On a smaller scale, I understand their wonder. They must have felt the same surge of awe as their ships approached new lands.

At exactly 11:00, Juan reported that Hermes had entered Europa's orbit and initiated the landing sequence. We held our collective breath. No craft had ever landed on this surface, which was rough and uneven based on all known data. We were concerned the landing might be a disaster.

Although Hermes' environmental data appeared nominal, uncertainty lingered among the team. Juan reported, "The weather appears as perfect as possible in an unknown environment. There are no swirling wind currents, no rain or sandstorms. This should be a breeze."

Everyone laughed at Juan's reference to the wind.

Juan sent his final landing instructions to the AI. He turned his head toward us and raised his hands, saying, "OK, let's see how the AI handles the touchdown."

As Hermes descended, Juan read out the incoming data: descending speed, pitch, roll, and potential issues, fifty meters, thirty meters, five meters.

Suddenly, Juan turned to us, his face calm and pleasant. The silence was almost overwhelming. Finally, he smiled and said, "Hermes has landed safely. Vector and Gene, she's yours now."

A great cheer erupted; all anxiety dissipated.

Vector and Gene were stationed at their consoles, ready to control Hermes and its robot, Rover.

The excitement of the launch washed away the tension between them. Both were smiling, brimming with anticipation as they prepared for the mission. Gene turned to her left and smiled at Vector, saying, "Are we ready?"

Vector just nodded, turning back to his task.

Vector began running diagnostics on Hermes, carefully verifying that its sample extraction systems were fully operational. At the same time, Gene conducted a parallel check on Rover, ensuring its functions were calibrated and ready.

Once both were satisfied, Vector uploaded the final set of instructions, transferring operational control to the onboard AI. The program directed Hermes and Rover to remain on Europa's surface until every assigned task was complete. Afterward, Hermes would ignite its engines, ascend from Europa, and begin the transit to Ares Haven Colony, where the collected samples would undergo detailed analysis.

Vector and Gene calculated it would take five days to achieve the sample collection goals.

They would monitor Hermes' and Rover's progress. Ready to intervene if problems arise. This oversight would continue as we traversed toward the Heliosphere.

Vector and Gene turned to their respective consoles and began sending instructions.

One hour after landing, Gene confirmed the robot had been deployed from the underside of Hermes.

Vector followed Gene's report, saying, "All systems are go for Hermes to begin its mission. It has begun drilling into the surface to extract ice, water, and additional minerals."

Within twenty minutes, both Gene and Vector confirmed data collection had begun.

Sitting near his console, Buzz turned to everyone in the room and said, "We will remain in the area for one day to ensure Hermes and Rover are functioning properly before continuing our journey. Gene and Vector keep a close eye on Hermes's transmission; we do not want to miss any data."

Turning to Juan, Buzz said, "Juan, you will be on hot standby in case we need to extract Hermes."

The excitement had faded, leaving behind a quiet stillness. I drifted toward the port-side windows, drawn by the silence beyond the glass. And then I saw it.
Europa.

It glowed against the blackness of space, a luminous orb wrapped in a bluish sheen, streaked with veins of reddish-brown; traces of salt and other minerals etched across its frozen surface. For a moment, my breath caught. I couldn't look away.

A smile tugged at my lips as I let myself imagine it the crunch of that alien ice beneath my boots, the first step onto a world that had waited eons for a visitor.

A few hours after Hermes' landing, Vector and Gene confirmed Hermes and Rover were functioning as programmed.

We all gathered in the galley, consuming our meal with great satisfaction. Excitement permeated throughout.

Slowly, we migrated to our berths to rest and re-energize for tomorrow. This has been the most exciting day for the team since leaving Mars. One small whiskey, and off to bed for me.

I close by reflecting on our travels thus far and wondering what the team's morale might have been if we had not been distracted by events along the way. We visited Luna and Ares Colonies, the Bounty incident, the Psyche asteroid, and now Hermes.

Hermes' data should keep us busy for some time. I often think of the God Particle, wondering if, after all of these adventures, the team is losing its excitement for this mission.

Closing my eyes, a quiet emptiness stirs within me, a gentle echo of the questions that linger: Does God exist? What truly happens when we die? These thoughts pull at me, leaving a strange, disjointed feeling, like a soft tug between fear and wonder, between the known and the unknowable. A chill overcomes me. With a slight shiver, I let those thoughts drift past, like clouds over a vast night sky. I do not need answers tonight. Tonight, I simply rest, carrying the mystery with me, and will allow sleep to cradle me until the light of morning.

EUROPA NEAR DISASTER

December 12th, 2036

At the crack of dawn, our team was abruptly awakened by blaring alarms echoing throughout the ship. I jumped out of my rack, wearing only shorts, and ran to the control room.

Along the way, Buzz and I collided, both falling to the ground. In that moment of chaos, sitting against the bulkhead, we looked at each other and laughed. A typical human reaction in a crisis. We stood and completed our sprint into the control room. Vector and Gene were already seated at their consoles, analyzing what happened.

Standing beside me, Buzz said, "Kelvin, turn off that alarm and flashing lights."

I sat at my console, found the alarm switch, and flipped it to the off position.

Without turning away from her console, Gene, in her typical analytical voice, said, "The alarm is from the Hermes. Vector, can you figure out what has gone wrong?"

Sitting at his console, Vector nodded and began frantically typing instructions into the computer.

He stopped keying, rose from his chair, and turned to us. His voice was calm, but the concern behind it was unmistakable.

"We may have a serious problem. During the night, the ground around the landing zone shifted. Hermes has tipped off-center. I need to determine just how far off vertical she is."

Without waiting for a reply, he pivoted back to his console, fingers flying as he pulled up the data.

Minutes dragged by until Vector finally swiveled in his seat, his expression grim.

"Hermes was drilling, attempting to trigger a steam geyser. The desire was to push water to the surface and gather samples. The geyser expanded faster than our simulations predicted. The ground gave way near Hermes."

He paused, the weight of his words hanging in the air. "We need eyes on this immediately."

Turning back to the console, Vector activated Hermes' external cameras to assess the damage.

Standing just behind Vector, I watched as Hermes' camera flickered to life. The image wavered, then steadied on a jagged slab of white crystal, the fuselage pressed against it at an awkward angle. My throat tightened. If Hermes was crippled, the mission might be over before it even began.

Vector said nothing. He kept shifting the camera's view, testing different angles, zooming in on scorched metal and shadowed joints. The room grew silent except for the faint hum of the monitors. I realized I was holding my breath.

Minutes crawled by, each one heavier than the last. I caught Gene drumming her fingers against the console, stopping when she noticed my look of concern. She grimaced. No one dared interrupt Vector's work.

At last, Vector leaned closer, froze the image, and let out a long breath. Relief softened his shoulders. He turned toward Gene, a faint smile tugging at his mouth. Pointing at the image on the screen, "We caught a break," he said. "She landed against a rock wall. It kept her from going all the way over. Hermes is holding at a forty-five."

The words lifted the weight in the room like a hatch opening. I hadn't realized how hard my heart had been pounding until it finally slowed.

Buzz immediately rallied the team to brainstorm the best approach for up-righting Hermes and resuming the mission. There were plenty of ideas.

One suggestion was to try firing the rockets on the side closest to the rock wall.

"There's too much risk with the engines," Theo said sharply. "If the firing angle is off, the section resting on the wall could be damaged."

After a short discussion, we agreed that this was not the ideal solution.

Theo leaned toward Gene with a devilish grin, a chuckle rumbling in his chest.
"You've been bragging nonstop about how versatile Rover is and how she can do anything. Well, why not prove it? Use Rover to get Hermes upright. Let's see that dog work."

A low grunt of agreement rolled across the room, followed by grins and nodding heads. The idea clicked instantly; simple, clever, and just crazy enough to work.

Gene stayed still, eyes narrowing as she ran through the possibilities. Then, with a sudden slap of her palm against the console, she broke the silence. "Piece of cake."

Looking down at her console, she began sending instructions to Rover, her fingers rapidly flowing over the keyboard. Suddenly, an audible dog barking sound could be heard over the intercom. Gene laughed, "Now this dog does hunt."

Laughter erupted throughout the control room, relieving the tension that had engulfed the team.

We stood behind Gene, watching on the monitors as she maneuvered Rover into position between Hermes and the rock base.

With Rover strategically positioned between Hermes and the rock base, Gene skillfully guided the robot's arms to the middle section of the crossbeam supporting Hermes' legs.

Gene smiled, saying, "gotcha. Now let's see if we can get Hermes upright."

A slow, meticulous dance began. Gene steadily moved Rover's appendage upward, gradually separating Hermes from the rock base.

We held our collective breath as we watched Hermes inch back into an upright position. As Hermes' suspended legs made contact with the ground, it began to sway. For a moment, we feared it might topple over in the opposite direction.

Hermes briefly swayed from side to side and then settled its four legs firmly on the ground.

Gene turned, triumphantly smiling, and said, "See a piece of cake?" She chuckled as she looked down at her console and returned to her work.

Buzz inquired, "How can we be sure Hermes can still perform its sample collection and launch to Mars?"

Vector replied, "Gene and I will run a complete

diagnostics. If all goes well, we will instruct Hermes to begin drilling again."

We patiently waited for the analysis to be completed. After twenty minutes, Vector and Gene had completed the diagnostic checks of both craft.

Vector reported to the team, "All systems are functioning nominally. Now it is time to see if Hermes can drill and extract samples."

He sat in silence, his face filled with concentration. Anxiety filled the room as we impatiently watched, anticipating the drilling to begin.

Suddenly, a cheer erupted, breaking the tension that had gripped the room. On the screen, we watched as Hermes's drill extended and bit into Europa's frozen surface.

Vector's console flared to life. Data lines cascaded as the drill penetrated deeper, reporting depth, resistance, and the first hints of minerals locked within the ice.

Every update felt monumental, and each data point was a step closer to unraveling Europa's secrets.

Vector's hands hovered above the keyboard, steady but taut, ready to intervene at the slightest anomaly. The room had fallen into reverent silence, broken only by the low hum of the machinery and the measured beeps of the console, echoing in the stillness like a heartbeat of progress.

"How's it looking, Vector?" Juan asked, breaking the silence.

Vector didn't look up, his eyes glued to the screen. "So far, so good. Hermes is stable, and the instruments are reading nominal."

Gene, standing nearby, nodded in agreement. "We've been waiting for this moment for a long time. Let's make it count."

The team exchanged glances, their faces reflecting relief. The success of their mission hinged on these crucial moments, and they were ready to give it their all.

Vector stood, stretching with both hands, and said, "I have sent the final instructions to the computer. It will ensure Hermes completes its tasks, collects Rover, and heads to Mars. We'll continue monitoring the mission, of course."

That evening, we celebrated our success with cigars and the whiskey provided by Bounty's captain.

Days like this make me feel fully alive. There's nothing like a crisis to stir the mind, test our ability to maintain calm in calamity, and devise and implement a solution. That isn't to say that nerves aren't frayed afterward. So, we settled down with a sip of whiskey, savoring the victory.

We will depart Europa tomorrow and race on to the Heliosphere and maybe the God Particle. I will sleep well tonight.

DEPARTING EUROPA

December 14th, 2036

Today, as we sailed past Europa, leaving Hermes and the rover to complete their mission, Gene and Vector continued monitoring the exploration progress, ensuring all programmed mission parameters would be met.

Our next waypoint is set for Saturn. The team had identified its moon, Titan, as a prime location for data collection and experiments. However, while reviewing our projected trajectory to the Milky Way, I discovered a significant problem with transiting to Titan.

Turning in my seat, with concern in my voice, "We cannot go to Titan. Based on Saturn's current orbiting position and our current course, we would have to make a 90% course correction. This would delay our mission to the Heliosphere and the God Particle by an additional two years. I recommend we stay on course and head to our primary objective."

Buzz spoke first. "I don't know about the rest of the team, but I vote to remain on our current course. We have been diverted from our mission long enough. No more course changes for Space Command!"

Gene, Juan, Theo, and I said, almost simultaneously, "Yes."

Vector wheeled around in his chair, quickly stood, and shouted, "Are you kidding me? I've spent the past two weeks and many sleepless nights developing experiments specifically designed for Titan. I vote we deviate from our current course and go to Titan!"

Knowing he was the only dissenter, Vector stood, punched the back of his chair and stormed out of the control room.

I yelled after him, "Vector, wait! There is an alternative that may interest you."

He stopped, turned to me with a sneer, "What?"

I began, "Can you adjust your Titan experiments? While reviewing our projected course, I realized Uranus lies directly along our path to the Heliosphere. We should reach it in about six and a half years. Would that give you enough time to modify your testing parameters for research on Uranus? If so, none of your work will go to waste."

Vector stood in the hatchway, contemplating my comments. After about two minutes, he began laughing out loud. He turned and smiled, "Heck yes. I'd better get started."

He walked back to his console, sat down, and began keying in ideas to modify his programs.

Buzz said, "Okay, it's settled. Juan, maintain our current course. On to Uranus and beyond."

Everyone went back to work.

Theo and I spent the remainder of the day searching for anomalies. Theo pointed at his monitor, saying, "Look at this. Is that a debris field?"

Turning to my left, looking over his shoulder, I replied, "Yes. I wonder how close we will come to its path."

The ship's advanced radar displayed tiny fragments barely registered, flickering in and out like static, but the larger masses stood out as dense, jagged clusters. To the trained eye, the display looked less like a star map and more like a swarm of predators circling unseen, paths overlapping, converging, diverging in a dance of chaotic motion. The radar sweep revealed the true scale: not an empty void, but a storm of stone and metal adrift in silence.

Theo tapped the screen, "Look at the size of the larger pieces. Large enough to possibly land a probe on and collect samples."

Utilizing radar and infrared imaging tools, Theo confirmed his estimation. These floating masses could easily hold the probe.

Massive rectangular slabs, some measuring twenty meters by thirty, drifted through the void. Black as obsidian, the surface swallowed light. Tiny flecks of glitter scattered across it shimmered like trapped stars, hinting at something both beautiful and unsettling.

Quickly turning back to my console, I did some quick calculations; turning to my left, I excitedly exclaimed, "Theo, utilizing our current course and speed, I project we will be within range of the field in five days."

"I believe the debris was left by a meteorite that passed this way sometime ago. We may have an opportunity to examine the field and collect samples."

Buzz turned in his chair and stood, saying, "It is time for our afternoon status reports. Let's get to the briefing room. This will be a perfect time to discuss your findings."

After everyone migrated to a seat, Buzz said, "Okay, to be sure we are all on the same page, I need to know what each member's plans are for today and moving forward."

I spoke first, "While searching for anomalies, Theo and I discovered a debris field that appears to be tail remains from a meteor. We picked up radioactive readings. We will be passing near the field in five days. Theo and I are planning to collect samples as we cruise by. Secondly, with the equipment on board, we should be able to get some interesting data to analyze.

Turning to Juan, I said, "Just as a heads up, you may need to adjust our course. Besides the debris field discovered, we have identified what appears to be a black hole near our plotted course. This needs to be watched. Provided there is no danger to us, Theo and I would like an opportunity to study it and collect as much data as possible. We would be the first scientists to get up close access to this scientific wonder. The sky is the limit for collecting data."

Buzz replied, "Ok. Juan will be on hot standby once we get close." Gene and Vector, your primary mission is to continue monitoring Hermes and its rover progress. This is day two of Hermes' five-day mission before departing for Ares Haven Colony."

Gene reported, "There have been some severe sandstorms near the Hermes landing site. This is causing short communications delays."

Vector followed up reporting, "Based on the last weather report, the storms on Europa should pass in the next twenty-four hours. Hermes will have sufficient power to complete the mission and fly to Mars."

Buzz added, "All sounds great. As for Juan and me, we will be performing routine maintenance, ensuring the ship is prepared for anything that may come our way. We still have a long way to go, and the ship must be functioning at its peak."

We left the briefing room full of energy and excitement as each team member returned to their respective assignments.

Tonight, here in my quarters, I sit in the silence, excitement humming beneath the stillness. Tomorrow holds unknown revelations.   But for now, sleep calls, and I surrender to its pull.

WONDERS OF SPACE

December 17th, 2036

For the past three days, our team has diligently prepared to gather extensive data from the meteorite's debris field.

For the first time in human history, mankind will have the opportunity to examine a meteorite's debris field closely. This unprecedented access to ancient cosmic materials, untouched for millennia, could lead to groundbreaking discoveries.

Side note, I still hate the sonic showers.

I walked into the galley to grab a cup of coffee. Juan sat looking out the port window, in deep contemplation. I asked him, "Where is everyone?"

He responded, "The team was so excited to start discussing the debris field that they grabbed their coffee or tea and made a beeline for the briefing room."

He laughed, "Let's go. Buzz asked me to gather you up once you arrived here."

Entering the briefing room, Buzz looked up and said, "Good afternoon. I'm glad to see you could make it." Everyone laughed. Now that you have graced us with your presence, we can get started."

With a sheepish grin, I quickly went and sat next to Theo.

Buzz began, "Given that this is uncharted territory for any

spacecraft, taking God Speed directly into the field would be too dangerous. I'm looking for alternatives allowing us to collect samples and bring them on board for analysis."

Juan cleared his throat, "We have a science probe onboard specifically designed for this purpose. There's no risk to us or God Speed. It can be remotely controlled and programmed to collect the desired samples."

Turning to Theo, he continued, "Theo, I'll be busy piloting God Speed to maintain our position. Didn't you receive extensive training on these probes?"

Theo's face lit up with excitement. "Yes, sir. I spent months training before leaving Earth. I've often wondered if I'd ever have an opportunity to take her for a spin."

Buzz nodded. "Alright, we should be within range to launch the probe in a few days.   Theo will control the probe, and Juan will maintain our station.   Everyone else should be at their consoles, collecting data and providing assistance as needed."

We slowly departed the briefing room, heading to our consoles to calibrate our instruments in anticipation of this exciting adventure.

As we drew closer to the field, Theo's voice crackled through the comms, charged with excitement.

"My instruments are picking up radioactive isotopes; uranium, thorium, potassium, aluminum, even traces of beryllium. And that's not all. I'm also detecting iron-nickel alloys, trilobite, and chromite deposits."

He paused only long enough to let the data scroll across his console before adding,
"These isotopes could be invaluable. They might reveal not only the age and history of this meteorite, but also how long it's been exposed to cosmic radiation. This could be a window into the deep past of the solar system itself."

Everyone refocused on their instruments. Suddenly, Theo jumped up from his console and shouted, "There's an isotope reading that doesn't fall within the known spectrum. Do any of you realize what this means?"

We shook our heads. Theo continued, "If the readings are correct, we may have just discovered a new radioactive isotope—a new element for the periodic table. I'll know more once we arrive on-site and collect samples."

Theo's excitement was contagious, spilling over to the rest of the crew. His voice carried an energy that made the sterile cabin feel alive as he outlined his findings and the potential discovery awaiting us. The thought of unearthing something entirely new electrified the mission, transforming routine exploration into the edge of revelation. Anticipation swelled with every passing hour. Juan's estimate of two days felt both tantalizingly close and unbearably distant.

Our team, reinvigorated by the prospect of groundbreaking science, refocused on its tasks. Each of us silently contemplated the significance of what we might uncover. The following forty-eight hours would be crucial, and our instruments must be ready to capture every detail.

Amid the excitement, it suddenly dawned on me to check on the Hermes project. I turned to Gene and asked, "Hey, what about Hermes? Are there any updates?"

Gene reported, "Hermes and Rover are functioning nominally. Both devices worked through their program instructions and are collecting many samples. Hopefully, the information extracted from the samples will go a long way toward determining the viability of life on Europa."

Hearing that was a relief. The data being collected could be groundbreaking. Given the delicate nature of the mission, every bit of information could be crucial for our understanding of Europa and the potential for life there.

I asked Gene, "Can you share more details about the type of samples Hermes is collecting and what we might be expected to find?"

She turned to me with a smile. "Hermes is focused on collecting ice core samples from the surface and drilling into the subsurface. We're searching for traces of microbial life, organic compounds, and any anomalous chemical signatures that could hint at biological activity. Beyond that, the samples will be sent to Ares Haven, where the mineral content will be analyzed to piece together Europa's geological history."

The thought of potentially discovering life or learning more about Europa's geology was exhilarating. With everything going on, it is easy to forget about the smaller steps in the larger mission, but each one was just as important as the last.

We spent the remainder of the day much to ourselves, collecting data or relaxing and contemplating what may lie ahead in a few days.

Gene and I sat in the galley, staring into the darkness of space, discussing the possible significance of finding the God Particle. If it is discovered, how will it impact our lives? Is there a deity or God? Will we survive the encounter?

She turned to me, worry etched on her face, asking, "How will we be able to explain being in the presence of God if that is the case?"

I shook my head, "As you know, I am an atheist; if anything, it might be an alien species, more advanced than humans."

Gene laughed, "Heck, we may not even make it there."

We said good night, departed the galley, and headed for our berths.

Our journey through the vastness of space presents unique challenges, particularly in maintaining a regular sleep schedule. The absence of natural light cues can disrupt our internal clock or circadian rhythm, making it challenging to stay synchronized. To address this, we have implemented various methods to simulate the natural progression of day and night, ensuring our bodies can adjust to the new environment.

One effective method is the use of controlled lighting in our living spaces. The bedrooms are equipped with a lighting system that gradually dims to mimic sunset, eventually going utterly dark as it would during nighttime on Earth. This helps signal our bodies that it is time to wind down and prepare for sleep. In the morning, the lights gradually brighten, simulating a sunrise and helping us to wake up naturally.

If I maintain a steady routine, my mind stays sharper, clearer, almost in rhythm with the ship's pulse. But drifting through the void of space has its own rules, and sometimes sleep feels more like an inconvenience than a necessity. I suspect I'm not the only one on the crew wrestling with that dilemma.

There's still a long journey ahead before we reach our destination. Focus must remain our constant companion. For now, though, a small measure of whiskey and then off to Wonderland.

METEORITE DEBRIS FIELD

December 19th, 2036

Today marked one of the most exciting and perhaps most demanding days since our departure from Mars. Two long-awaited projects were finally reaching fruition, and the anticipation had settled over the ship like a quiet electric charge.

After enduring the usual half-hearted rinse from the sonic shower and rewarding myself with a proper shave, I felt halfway human again. The scent of recycled air clung faintly to my skin as I descended the corridor toward the galley, the hum of the ship's systems steady in the background.

The familiar aroma of eggs and coffee greeted me when I stepped through the hatch into the galley.

Theo and Gene were already there, seated across from each other, plates half-empty. Their voices carried the intensity reserved for a day that mattered. They leaned in close, trading plans and theories in quick bursts, the low murmur of their conversation hinting at the excitement ahead.

Vector, already seated beside Juan, waved me over with a grin. I slid into the chair, and soon our conversation buzzed with speculation about the day's missions; each of us trading theories and expectations with the eagerness of gamblers about to roll the dice.

I had just finished the last bite of my meal when Buzz appeared in the doorway, his tone brisk and commanding.

"Everyone to the briefing room. We've got a full plate today. Let's get the briefing done and move on to the tasks at hand."

Moments later, we were gathered in the briefing room, the air charged with anticipation. Hermes' progress and the assignments for the meteorite debris project filled the agenda, each detail sharpening the sense that today would matter.

Theo piloted the probe into the debris field. He looked around the room with a knowing smirk, saying, "I have named the probe Icarus. Let's hope it does not burn up in flight." Everyone chuckled, understanding the mythical story of Icarus and how he flew too close to the sun, melting his wings and crashing. He said, "The name symbolizes humanity's unending quest for knowledge and the desire to venture into the unknown."

Icarus is compact yet rugged, designed to survive the harshest environments of deep space and planetary surfaces. Its main body was a hexagonal chassis, armored in lightweight titanium alloy panels coated with a thermal-protective finish. At its core lay the power system: a small nuclear battery supplemented by deployable solar arrays, which extended outward like angular wings to catch whatever sunlight was available.

Clusters of wide-angle and microscopic cameras surround it, giving the probe sharp vision from sweeping panoramas to close-up textures of dust grains.

Extending from one side was the primary robotic arm, jointed and dexterous, tipped with a modular toolkit: a scoop, a coring drill, and a precision gripper. Near its base was a rotating carousel of sealed sample containers, each capable of locking away fragments of soil or ice in pristine condition. On the opposite side sat a deployable spectrometer array, capable of analyzing chemical composition on the spot, while ground-penetrating radar antennas folded neatly beneath the belly of the craft.

Four of the landing legs were shock-absorbing struts capped with broad, circular foot pads, engineered to keep the probe steady on uneven or soft terrain. Compact thrusters and attitude control jets dotted the frame, subtle reminders of its journey from orbit to surface.

Utilizing the data collected during our journey to the site, Theo pinpointed the exact locations within the debris field to collect the desired samples. His primary focus would be to gather known isotopes. The samples will be used to estimate the meteorite's age and possibly identify its place of origin.

Additionally, Theo would attempt to extract the unknown isotopes and determine if it truly represented a new discovery. He smiled, saying, "If this element does not fall within any known isotope spectrum."

He boldly declared, "I, as the discoverer, will have the honor of naming it and adding its number to the periodic table."

A universal chuckle erupted as Buzz quipped, "Only you, Theo, would be so bold." Theo stood and took a bow.

Buzz continued, "Based on our course and speed, we should be within the agreed-upon safe distance from the field by 1300."

While element chasing was being discussed, Juan and Gene solidified their plan to retrieve Hermes and Rover. They needed to get Rover back on board Hermes, secure the cargo, and launch Hermes on its trajectory to Mars.

Gene said, "I will be responsible for Rover getting back to Hermes, loaded and secured for takeoff. Based on its current location, it will be safely snuggled into Hermes within an hour."

Juan added, "By then, I will have ensured Hermes drilling has stopped, completed onboard per-launch protocols, and be ready for launch. Once Hermes has safely exited Europa's atmosphere, I will notify Ares Haven that Hermes has launched and is en route. The final piece will be confirmation from the Colony that they have operational control."

At 1315, Buzz guided us within fifty kilometers of the debris. Sitting in the pilot's seat, he turned to Theo and said, "Okay, it's all yours. Because of the instability of the field, I cannot risk getting any closer."

Theo smiled, nodded, turned to his console, took a deep breath, and said, "Let's go get our samples."

Reaching to his left, he latched onto Icarus' controls and launched it toward the debris field. He had programmed the course coordinates into Icarus.

Through Icarus' onboard cameras, Theo watched its steady crawl toward the field, every flicker of light across its lens carrying a promise of discovery. Once positioned in the debris field, Icarus would transmit images of the rocks it flagged as holding the precious materials, each picture a potential breakthrough for the waiting crew.

Looking out the forward portal, It was almost surreal watching Icarus gracefully and methodically navigate through the field. It maneuvered itself, selecting only the desired samples and placing them within its cargo hold.

Suddenly, I saw the craft begin violently swerving from its course as if something had struck it. I quickly turned to Theo and, with a look of panic on my face, yelled, "Icarus is flying erratically; something is wrong."

Theo quickly turned to the console, confirming Icarus was off course and spinning out of control. Someone yelled, "What the heck just happened?" There was no reply.

Theo switched Icarus's controls to manual override. Grimacing with sweat pouring down his face, he worked frantically to get the craft back under control and on course.

In a strained voice, Theo mumbled, "If I do not get this under control quickly, Icarus will eventually crash into the debris and be destroyed."

Buzz sat in his pilot seat, keeping God Speed stationary. In his usual calm, commanding voice, He called back to Theo, "Let me know what you need from us. I have God Speed under control. Say the word if we need to close on the field to assist the recovery."

Theo calmly replied, "Roger, I will advise."

Vector stood behind Theo and placed a reassuring hand on his shoulder.

With a placid face, Theo began reading incoming data on Icarus's health. "Thrusters are offline, engine igniting sporadically, and the pitch control fins are not deployed. A total out of control is the result. The problem is with the propulsion system, causing it to fly out of control."

Theo looked to his left. Warning lights were flashing, indicating a minor hull breach had occurred. He yelled, "Crap, we also have a hull breach. Vector, can you determine the severity of the breach?"

As Theo worked diligently to stabilize Icarus, Vector turned and sat at a second console next to Theo. With the concentration of a surgeon, he read incoming data to assess the severity of the breach and whether the damage was critical.

Both men operated in controlled chaos, trying to return Icarus to a nominal state. The strain on each man's face was evident.

Vector reported, "The breach in the hull appears minor, with no real structural damage. As for your out-of-control probe, I recommend shutting down the engines for a restart to stabilize Icarus."

Theo turned to Vector with clenched teeth, nodded, and replied, "Roger, that's the only solution that makes sense."

Theo turned back to the controls and hit the shutdown

button. In a subdued voice, he declared, "Shutdown is complete." He threw himself back into his seat, took a deep breath, and gathered his composure for the next step: restarting the engines. He mumbled, "I hope this works; otherwise, all the planning I have done will be for nothing."

I watched from the portal window as Icarus's engines went dark. Now, floating aimlessly in space, just another piece of space debris.

Theo and Vector sat at their consoles anxiously reviewing the data to determine how long to wait before restarting.

The phrase by Benjamin Franklin, "A watch pot never boils", is apropos here. We agonizingly stood idle, as time ticked by, waiting for Theo to reignite the engines. All were hoping Icarus would again be in a nominal state.

Theo looked down at his readings, confirming it had stabilized.

Three minutes had passed since the engine shutdown; it felt like an eternity. Theo looked at Vector, crossed his fingers, and said, "Well, it's time. Here's hoping the restart solves the problem."

Vector could only nod. Theo counted down, "Three, two, one." He gently flipped the restart button, afraid of what might come next. We collectively held our breath, staring at the monitors, willing Icarus's engines to start and stabilize.

Gene watched from the portal window as Iricus floated aimlessly within the field, showing no sign of life. The rest of the team stared at Icarus's onboard cameras.

For a moment, there was nothing. A small flame suddenly burst onto our screen, confirming that Iricus's engines had fired up.

"Engine restart successful," Vector reported, his voice filled with relief. "All systems are nominal."

Everyone began to cheer.

Theo turned to the console and adjusted the thrusters until the craft was flying smoothly and ready to complete its mission.

Gene stared out into the abyss, Icarus's shiny hull floating barely visible. Watching the scene unfold, she smiled. She turned to Theo and said, "It looks like Icarus has stopped the radical swaying."

Vector reviewed the incoming data on the craft's health. Relief was evident in Vector's voice and face. With a vast smile turned to Theo, saying, "Icarus is healthy and ready to resume sample collection."

There was a great sigh of relief heard throughout the ship.

Theo thrust himself back into his chair, took a deep breath, and said, "Now, let's go get our samples."

After the chaos subsided, a thought occurred to me. What about the Hermes launch? I looked around the control room for Juan and Gene. Both were seated on the far side of the room, preparing to initiate Rover's recovery and Hermes launch. Juan kept a sharp eye on Hermes, utilizing the onboard cameras, while Gene monitored Rover's progress. They discussed their plan to get Rover back and load it onto Hermes.

Gene's responsibility was to get the Rover back to Hermes. She turned to Juan and said, "I am having a problem communicating with the rover. It traversed behind a rock formation, causing a delay with the instructions I am sending."

After a stressful hour of navigating Rover through the rock formation, Gene was able to move Rover to Hermes' location.

Juan monitored Hermes's onboard cameras, searching for Rover. An hour after Gene reported Rover was moving toward Hermes, Juan pointed at Hermes' port-side camera, smiled, turned toward Gene, and reported, "Gene, I can see

Rover closing on Hermes."

Gene replied, "Well, based on Rover's speed capability and distance, it will take two hours to get to Hermes. You might as well take a break. I will monitor the progress.

Juan stood, stretching his legs. As he walked away, he said, "Hermes systems are nominal. We need only wait for Rover to return. Gene, let me know when Rover arrives. I will be in the galley."

Gene replied, "Roger."

While Gene and Juan worked to complete the Hermes mission, Theo maneuvered Icarus through the debris field, selecting the samples for collection. He called out the sample identification as each was secured into Icarus's storage bay.

Theo's excitement was electric, almost contagious, as he turned to Vector with a grin. "Now for the final sample. Keep an eye on the radiation levels. I believe this is the unknown isotopes."

Vector nodded, his eyes already glued to the monitor displaying the radiation levels. "Got it, Theo. I'll keep a close watch."

Theo's hands trembled slightly as he carefully maneuvered Icarus toward a large rock fifteen by twenty meters—large enough to land and collect the identified sample.

This was tricky to perform. If not performed correctly, landing on a large surface as it moved through space could result in disaster.

Theo expertly maneuvered Icarus onto the rock, softly landing exactly where the unknown element had been located.

A three-meter by three-meter hole had been punched through the rock, revealing the raw shimmer of the exposed element. Theo drew in a steadying breath, gripped the controls, and guided the robotic arm with painstaking precision toward the sample. The room fell into a hushed intensity, the entire team leaning forward, eyes locked on the feed. Instruments flared with rising readings, registering radiation levels well beyond normal, a telltale signal that the unknown isotopes were present.

Theo grasped the sample, slowly contracted the robotic arm, and gently placed it into Icarus' cargo bay. He let out a sigh of relief, knowing he had successfully collected the desired sample. "Perfect. This could be a significant discovery, " he said to no one in particular.

Vector looked puzzled. He loudly announced, "The isotope readings in this sample do not match any known on the EM spectrum."

Buzz, standing nearby, clapped Theo on the back. "Great work, everyone. Let's get Icarus back on board and see what we've got. This could be the breakthrough you've been waiting for."

Theo stood with a huge smile, shouting, "If this is a new element, we must think of a proper name."

Buzz responded, "Let's not get ahead of ourselves. Do the science, then make the claim."

Within an hour, Icarus returned and docked with God Speed.

Vector and Theo exhaled a great sigh of relief. Theo stood from his console and bowed his head in fatigue, saying, "I am bushed. We should begin analyzing the samples tomorrow. I am getting something to eat, then to my rack for a good night's sleep."

Vector smiled, rose from his console, and slowly trailed behind Theo.

Just as Juan exited the control room, Instruments on his console began to flash and beep. Walking back to the console, Juan turned off the warning lights and alarm. He turned to his left, saw Gene staring, daydreaming out of the portal window, and said, "Gene, Rover has loaded itself on board Hermes. We are ready to launch."

Gene replied, "Coming." She sat down at her console, took a deep breath, and said, "Rover is secure within Hermes; everything is ready."

Juan looked down at his console and saw that Hermes' external cameras were functioning properly for the launch. He smiled and said, "We are a go." He counted down: three, two, one, and then depressed the launch button, sending a signal to Hermes to launch.

The cameras displayed the vibrations on Hermes' hull as she slowly lifted off from the surface.

I walked over and stood behind Juan. The video displayed the engines firing up, sending Hermes and her cargo through Europa's atmosphere and into space en route to Ares Colony.

Juan turned a knob on his console until it reached a radio frequency channel associated with Ares Haven. He keyed the microphone and called, "Ares, this is God Speed, over."

There was dead air as we patiently waited for a response. As usual, waiting for something to happen seems to take forever. Finally, Ares responded. "God Speed, this is Ares Haven over."

Juan announced, "Ares, this is God Speed. We have launched Hermes and set her course to Mars. Please confirm you are in communication with Hermes and have taken control."

Areas Haven responded, "Roger, God Speed, standby."

Silence followed. Tension filled the air as we impatiently waited for confirmation that Ares Haven had control.

Finally, after five minutes of nothing, Ares replied, "Roger, God Speed, we have taken control of Hermes. We anticipate her return flight will take approximately eight months. I will advise once she has returned. Good luck on your mission to find the God Particle."

An audible sigh of relief was heard throughout the control room. Juan exhaled, smiled, and signed off.

Looking around the control room, relief and satisfaction radiated from each member's face. Hermes had successfully recovered samples from Europa and was on its way, and Icarus had safely returned from its collection mission.

Tomorrow will be another exciting day. After a day like this, I will quickly fall asleep, satisfied with the day's adventures.

A NEW ELEMENT

December 20th, 2036

I woke refreshed after yesterday's excitement. I quickly jumped into an uninspiring sonic shower, dressed, and headed to the galley.

Walking into the galley, I was greeted by the rich aroma of freshly brewed coffee. The room was empty. I quickly poured myself a cup and headed to the briefing room.

Entering the room, the team huddled around the table deep in conversation.

Buzz glanced up with a smirk and quipped, "Good morning. Did you party too hard last night or stuck in a dream with your women, Elmo?"

The room erupted in laughter. I took a seat.

With excitement in his voice, Theo began sharing his findings on the elements: "Last night, I could not sleep. I sat at my console and ran an electromagnetic analysis on the samples. As I suspected, we have uranium, thorium, potassium, aluminum, and beryllium present."

He smiled and continued, "With these samples, I may be able to determine the age and origin of the meteorite that deposited the particles."

With a twinkle in his eyes and a barely contained thrill in his voice, Theo exclaimed,

" I may have stumbled onto something even more exciting. The EM analysis revealed an element with wavelengths spanning 300 to 900 nanometers. It behaves like a metal, yet its signature resembles that of Helium-3. It's perplexing."

My mind raced through possibilities of what this element could be used for faster than I could hold them.

Theo leaned forward, energized. "If I can confirm it shares Helium-3's properties but isn't a gas, we might be looking at a brand-new element."

I couldn't hold back. "Theo, do you realize what this means? If it proves true, Ares Haven may have an alternative fuel source for its fusion reactors. I want in on the analysis."

The room erupted in a low buzz of excitement, voices overlapping as everyone speculated. A new element, something to add to the Periodic Table. A stable, metallic alternative to Helium-3. The implications rippled outward: science, energy, colonization, the very future of space exploration.

Buzz's steady baritone cut through the chatter, re-anchoring us.

"Alright, this may be groundbreaking. But let's keep our

heads clear. First, we verify the analysis. Then we celebrate."

As everyone began leaving, Juan stood, saying, "One more thing. Gene and I plan to continue monitoring Hermes' transit to Ares Haven. This was our baby. We want to be sure it gets to its destination."

With a smile and a nod, Buzz replied, "Ok, get going."

Both Gene and Juan smiled, stood, and almost ran out of the room, excited to see Hermes's progress.

Theo turned to me, "Vector and I want to review some data before we start digging deeper into the sample analysis. Can you ensure our lab protective gear and analytical equipment are ready? This must be done before we move the samples into the lab."

Quickly turning, I commented, "No problem. I was getting stagnant, standing here needing something to do."

Entering the cargo bay, I walked to the adjacent lab, went to the gear closet, pulled down each piece of equipment, checking for damage.

After determining each suit and headgear were functioning correctly, my next goal; ensure the lab was ready. After an hour checking the lab equipment, I was satisfied all was in order.

Walking to the intercom system, depressed the transmit button and informed Theo that the protective gear and the equipment in the lab were ready.

Theo responded, "Roger. I'm finishing my review of the collected data. I'll use the electromagnetic array to confirm the material's wavelength and determine its atomic mass." When I returned to the control room, Theo's voice carried an edge of excitement. "The data looks promising," he said. "Vector, you and I need to gear up and move the samples to the lab. What do you say we go unpack our new delivery?"

Vector jumped up from his seat. "What are we waiting for?"

Vector and Theo entered the cargo bay, put on their protective gear, and moved the samples into the lab.

After completing this process, Theo said, "It has been a long morning. Let's go get something to eat and rest. We can take this up after lunch."

Looking fatigued, Vector grumbled, "I am really hangry." He removed his gear and headed for the galley.

Sitting in the galley, the team's conversation bubbled with speculation about whether Theo would become a Nobel Prize recipient, assuming he proved the unknown element wasn't on the periodic table.

Observing my colleagues, it struck me that Theo and all of us could be written into history books.

Smiling, I postulated whether we would be remembered forever, assuming we discovered the God Particle and survived.

Theo could be immortalized for his new element discovery.

My thoughts were broken by loud laughter. Vector stood in an exaggerated bow before Theo, declaring, "Oh, great and wise scientist, I am unworthy!"

Theo grinned, snatching a spatula from the counter and wielding it like a royal scepter. With mock solemnity, he tapped Vector's shoulders. "Sir Vector, arise. You may now assist me with my research."

Still smiling, he laid the spatula back down and strolled toward the lab.

Theo and Vector stepped into the lab, the faint hum of ventilation systems filling the sterile air. Vector gestured toward a reinforced table where the unknown elements rested, sealed behind a transparent, lead-lined glass partition. The samples lay within the clean room, their faint glimmer hinting at mysteries waiting to be uncovered. From the control station just outside the chamber, we could run diagnostics and monitor conditions without breaching containment, the protective barrier ensuring both safety and precision in our work.

Theo smiled, saying, "Let's get started." He turned on a recording device to document their research and began, "The sample is roughly 3 meters by 3 meters. It has a silvery-gray appearance. The surface is pocked in some areas, smooth, and shiny in others. We will perform several tests, including using a Geiger counter to identify radioactivity.

This will be followed by using an oscilloscope to identify the sample's position on the electromagnetic spectrum."

A mass spectrometer will then determine the element's atomic weight.

"Assuming this is a new element with characteristics similar to Helium-3, I will attempt to fuse the sample with deuterium. A second source to power Luna and Ares Haven Colony's fusion power plants."

Vector laughed excitedly, saying, "Hmmm, a new element?"

Theo flipped a switch, and the Geiger counter came alive with a sharp, steady crackle that filled the room. His eyes widened as he leaned closer to the gauge.
"Wow—look at that. It's pegged. No question, this sample is hot."

Without hesitation, he reached over with his left hand and powered up the oscilloscope. A steady and insistent green trace pulsed across the screen, registering a distinct band of radio waves.

Theo keyed the microphone, his voice tight with excitement. "The emission falls between 300 and 900 hertz. Fascinating… that's in the range we'd expect from Helium-3."

Turning to the console, Vector located the mass spectrometer switch. His voice filled with anticipation, he said, "Let's see what the mass spec has to say."

He flipped the switch. They stood hovering over the printer, awaiting the mass spec's analysis. Minutes slid by; the printer came alive, producing the anticipated report.

Theo, visibly shaking with excitement, pulled the report from the printer. Reading the report aloud, "It has an atomic mass of 181u, consisting of 90 protons and 91 neutrons. It is a NEW! Element."

He dashed back to the control center, shouting, "We've discovered a new element. The Periodic Table Number will be 127. I have named it Theonium-127. "

"Now we need to test our theory that 127 can be fused with deuterium. If successful, it could propel colonization far beyond Mars, opening the way to distant planets."

Cheers erupted around him as we congratulated Theo on his groundbreaking discovery.

Theo smiled, realizing his discovery had placed him in a new scientific stratosphere. He was one of the few who would have his name associated with the discovery of a new element on the periodic table.

Theo looked at Vector, somberly saying, "Are you ready? Let's make some energy."

A quick devilish smile flashed on Vector's face. As he raced back to the lab, he yelled back, "Let's get started."

Arriving quickly, Theo inserted his hands into protective gloves attached to the protective glass to begin the fusion experiment.

Reaching for a vacuum tube, Theo placed the Theonium-127 sample into one side and injected deuterium into the other side.

Suddenly, electrons from both elements fused, creating a massive energy spike. The glow in the lab was blinding for just a few seconds. Theo managed to contain the fusion energy in a secure vacuum tube.

Vector ran to the equipment, monitoring the energy. He excitedly screamed, "The meters are pegged and frozen at the final reading."

Realizing they had successfully fused Theonium-127 and deuterium, creating energy that could be replicated in the colonies' fusion power plants, Theo staggered back from the protective glass. He was speechless as he contemplated what had just happened.

With awe in his voice, Vector whispered, "Theo, we need to send this data to Ares Haven. The debris field will pass near Mars, allowing them to collect more Theonium-127. They will need to devise a plan to make this happen quickly."

Theo's face lit up with an ear-to-ear grin as he fully grasped the magnitude of their achievement.

As if waking from a dream, Theo thought, "I need to get to the data." As he read the reports spewing from the printer, he turned to Vector with an exuberant smile, took a deep breath, and softly spoke, "We have a new energy source for fusion power plants. I have never seen this much power when fusing elements."

Theo and Vector quickly compiled their findings and compressed the data for faster transmission.

I suggested we also send the data to Luna Colony and Earth to ensure Theo receives credit for his discovery. Everyone agreed, recognizing the importance of sharing this revolutionary advancement across all human settlements.

The discovery of Theonium-127 promised to revolutionize energy production and space exploration. With properties similar to Helium-3, it offers a new fuel source for fusion reactors, providing a clean, nearly limitless energy supply. Having a second source for fusion makes fusion propulsion systems in spacecraft more viable. It should also open the door to faster, more efficient interplanetary travel.

As the data packets were beamed to Mars, Luna, and Earth, Theo couldn't help but feel a profound sense of accomplishment. This moment marked not only a personal victory but also a giant leap forward in humanity's quest to harness the power of the stars.

The past two days have been exhilarating. When we left Earth, I worried our journey through space to chase the God Particle would be mundane. So far, that hadn't been the case.

Our next stop is a flyby of Uranus. We plan to conduct a flyby analysis and possibly send a probe to collect data for Space Command.

For now, I'll finish my Crown Royal and head to bed.

I was able to video conference with Elmo on Luna Colony. We discussed Theo's discovery and the positive impact it will have on any colony's power plants in the future.

    After closing with Elmo and watching the screen go dark, I sat in silence, the echo of her voice still lingering in my mind. Yet beneath the warmth of our exchange, an emptiness consumed me.

    As time ticks forward on this journey, I can't escape a thought that keeps surfacing: in all the meticulous planning for long-range missions, fuel reserves, life-support systems, radiation shielding, something vital has been overlooked. A true companion.

    Crew members share duties, stress, and even laughter, but do not fill that void. Companionship is not the same as camaraderie. One is forged in necessity, the other in something far deeper, a mutual belonging. I believe this absence must be addressed if humanity hopes to endure the silence of the stars.

    But for now, I must push past the emptiness and look forward to tomorrow.

ON TO URANUS

August 15th, 2041

It is remarkable how quickly time has passed, especially in scientific discovery. It has been six and one-half years since we collected samples from the debris field.

Since then, Theo and Vector have dedicated themselves to an exhaustive reanalysis of the retrieved materials. Their primary focus has been to prove the existence of Theonium-127 as a genuinely new element.

The scientific approach they employed was rigorous and methodical. Rather than simply trying to prove their initial findings, Theo and Vector adopted a strategy aimed at disproving their methods of creating a new element.

This approach is often referred to as falsification. It is a cornerstone of the scientific method. By attempting to invalidate their own results through various tests and experiments, they ensured that their conclusions were robust and reliable.

After months of painstaking work, exploring every conceivable method to disprove the properties of Theonium-127, Theo and Vector were ultimately unable to refute their findings.

This exhaustive process left them both satisfied with the validity of their discovery.

Theonium-127 has been confirmed as a new element, a testament to their dedication and the power of thorough scientific investigation.

Three years after our encounter with the debris field, Mars confirmed the debris field's path was within striking distance of the planet. Ares Haven had planned for this event and sent ships to collect every possible sample before the field moved beyond their reach.

At our morning briefing, Buzz spoke, "I hold in my hand a personal note from Ares Haven Commander, Jack Halsey, thanking the entire team for their efforts. Here is what he writes,"

'Because of the team's outstanding work, Ares Haven's power plant will have sufficient material to power the colony for decades. This would not have been possible without God Speed team's efforts. Thank you, Jack Halsey, Ares Haven.'

Buzz continued, "In about ten minutes, we should receive Ares Haven's and Space Command's final report surrounding Theonium-127. Let's move to the communications center."

We gathered in the communications center, impatiently waiting for the printer to come alive. Suddenly, the printer began translating the electronic transmissions into words.

As each page was filled, Buzz quickly pulled it from the printer and read the content. The first pages included messages filled with congratulations from scientists and heads of state confirming that Theonium-127 had been officially recognized as a new element.

Buzz commented, "It took them long enough."

He continued, "Research teams on Ares Haven have successfully repeated Theo's and Vector's groundbreaking experiment: the controlled fusion of deuterium with Theonium-127. Their results confirm the existence of Theonium-127 as a new element and validate Theo's pioneering work."

"Commander Halsey reported the fusion reaction generated an unprecedented surge of energy, surpassing every previous achievement in scientific history. The scale and efficiency of this breakthrough mark a decisive turning point for the colony."

Space Command leadership commented in the report, "With this advancement, Ares Haven is now positioned to power and sustain larger, more complex communities. The confirmation of Theonium-127's role in fusion technology not only secures the colony's energy future but also establishes Ares Haven as a center of innovation."

Further confirming Theonium-127's official addition to the Periodic Table and the submission of Theo's name for a Nobel Prize. They also inquired whether other team members should be included in the nomination.

Theo, beaming with pride and excitement, turned to Vector, who was seated next to him. With a hearty laugh, he said, "Well, my friend, I would like your name to be submitted with mine."

Vector, taken aback, his lips quivering with emotion, replied softly, "My friend, if you are certain. I would be proud to be mentioned as a minor contributor."

The entire team erupted in cheers, thrilled for both men and their well-deserved recognition.

Theo, still grinning, gave Vector a hearty hug, shaking him, smiling, and asking, "How does it feel to be famous?"

The room buzzed with energy, the team basking in the success and camaraderie of their shared achievement.

Vector looked around the room, glanced out of the portal into the abyss, and mumbled, "I guess we are famous here; there is no one else around."

An uproar of laughter filled the room.

Theo stood smiling, saying, "Team, unless anyone can think of a reason to retain the samples, I recommend we jettison them. We may need the space. "There were no objections.

Theo and Vector headed for the lab to jettison the samples into the abyss.

Juan shared additional news: "Late last night, Gene and I received communications from Ares Haven. Hermes had successfully landed at the colony. They had spent months analyzing the materials and confirmed that water could be extracted from the surface for drinking and conversion to consumable oxygen. They had transmitted their findings to Earth and sent Hermes to Space Command for final analysis."

Buzz took a deep breath and smiled, "Great news all around: this team's performance has exceeded anything Space Command had anticipated. Let's see how we perform when we reach our primary objective, the God Particle."

"If you look out the portal, you can see we are closing in on Uranus. We should be on station by the end of the day. Tomorrow, Gene and Kelvin will launch two probes to analyze the planet."

"The probes should maintain a distance of two hundred miles above the surface. As we know, Uranus is a gaseous, cyan-colored ice giant. The primary elements identified during previous probes' investigations were water, ammonia, and methane. We do not expect to find anything new, but we shall see.

Kelvin, Gene, go ahead and get to the control room to review launch protocols for tomorrow."

Gene and I spent the remainder of the day reviewing the launch protocols and discussing where each probe should be placed in Uranus' orbit for optimum data collection.

Once we finished, Gene turned to me and said, "Let's get a drink and call it a day." I replied, "I have a great single malt in my room." Gene nodded.

We spent the rest of the night discussing the God Particle, both wondering if this adventure would be worth what we might find. I wondered out loud, "What if this has been for nothing?" Silence filled the room as we both contemplated my last comment.

Around midnight, Gene touched my shoulder and, with a tired smile, said, "We have a full day tomorrow. I need some sleep." I stood, nodded, and walked her out.

As we get closer to our primary mission, searching for the God Particle, my apprehension about its success multiplies.

Although I have always been an atheist, there is a small hope that I am wrong and that God does exist. Then I may someday see my lovely daughter again.

   In crastinum problema est.   It is a problem for tomorrow.

URANUS

August 16th, 2041

Late this morning, we stationed God Speed in a high orbit above Uranus. Its appearance was precisely as Buzz had described. The surface was an awe-inspiring aqua, inviting explorers to come to the surface.

Gene and I sat at our control panels, running diagnostics to ensure the probes would run optimally.

Gene turned to me, "I looked over the data available from other probes. I cannot imagine we will find anything significant in this mission. This is a waste of our time. We should be on our way to the Heliosphere and searching for the God Particle."

Without lifting my head, I grumbled, "You are probably right; I am ready to get on with our mission."

Buzz was standing in the hatchway, listening to the conversation. He walked over to us, placed a hand on each of our shoulders, and said, "I know it may be a waste of time, but what else would we be doing to fill the gap until we get to the Heliosphere?"

Silence filled the space. Buzz turned, walked away, and said, "Well, alright."

Gene declared, "Ok, my probe is ready to launch."

I responded, "Yep, mine, too. Let's get this over with."

We simultaneously reached for the launch button. In a monotone voice, I began the countdown, "Ready! Three, two, one." Gene and I hit the launch buttons.

Turning on the cargo bay cameras, we steered each craft out into the abyss, setting a course to our designated target. The probe's onboard cameras transmitted images as they closed to the safe orbiting altitude of two hundred miles.

The images revealed a gray-blue desolate atmosphere. The alluring color seemed inviting, as if to say, "Come land here." The data informed us that anyone landing on its surface would inevitably be consumed by the poisonous gasses encompassing the planet.

The monitors began displaying data, confirming the probes were functioning correctly and collecting information.

After an hour of collecting data and comparing it to information obtained from probes previously sent to Uranus. Gene turned to me with a bored expression and said, "This is a waste of our time. Everything we have collected is similar to the historical data."

I turned to my console and, with a sigh, agreed. Picking up the intercom, I began speaking, "Buzz, we have been collecting data; there is nothing new to report. I recommend we recall the probes and continue chasing the God Particle."

Buzz and the Team walked into the control room. He could see our frustration and boredom. He looked at Gene and me, smiled, and said, "OK, let's get our probes back and be on our way."

There was an air of satisfaction throughout the room. We had become impatient and anxious, ready to complete our primary mission. There have been many late-night discussions about the God Particle. Each member has opinions and beliefs may be tested when encountering the God Particle, if it exists.

I am an atheist. Believing that once our being ceases to exist, our energy is consumed by the cosmos and reconstituted. After the loss of my daughter, there are days that I hope, just maybe, there is an afterlife so that I can see my lovely child again. But hope springs eternal; I am steadfast in my belief. No God, no afterlife.

Buzz and Juan are the quintessential military men who believe in God and Country. Buzz was born in the "Bible Belt" and grew up in a little country town in the West Virginia hills. Everyone attends church and praises God at least twice a week. God is the center of their community.

Juan was raised on the border in Texas. As with most Mexican families, God is the primary source of his strength. During our late-night discussions, neither man could be moved from believing God made the universe. Randomness does not exist. And when they pass beyond this life, they will be in the hereafter with family members who went before them.

Gene is an interesting woman. Raised Roman Catholic, she later embraced science and became agnostic. Her spiritual journey continued for many years, leading her to explore Buddhism.

One evening, during our discussions, she calmly said, "Buddhists believe that whether the God Particle exists or not, they know that until Nirvana is reached, reincarnation is the natural evolution." She looked at Buzz, laughing, and added, "Maybe I will come back as Buzz."

This was met with great laughter. Her expression turned somber as she looked around the room, saying, "My searches for an answer to whether there is a divine entity have left me with more questions than answers. I want to know more."

Vector believes there is nothing after life and subscribes to his cousins' beliefs. His comments include, "I have always tried to do everything I desire. After all, once we die, there is nothing. Our energy is repurposed for something entirely different."

He laughed and said, "I hope my energy is consumed by an alien." A great uproar consumed the galley.

Theo is an interesting character. He has yet to contribute to our galley conversations on the existence of God or a supreme being. He sits quietly, taking in the various points of view but never engages in the fray. We have done everything possible to encourage him, but have yet to succeed. Whatever he believes, he is not willing to share.

I wonder how finding the God Particle will impact our perspectives on our lives and beliefs. As a scientist, I am excited to delve into the possibilities, but as a human being, I have some trepidation.

What if we find nothing?

What if the particle exists?

Does God exist?"

This adventure may upend mankind's understanding of the universe and God.

Within two hours of deciding to end the Uranus data collection, Gene and I returned the probes and safely tucked them into the cargo bay.

Turning in my chair, I saw Buzz in his pilot chair,

concentrating on the console. I said, "Hey Buzz if you stare any harder at the screen, you may go blind."

Without lifting his head in a focused voice, he said, "I am plotting the best course to take us to the Heliosphere. No more distractions; I want to get this project started. We have been traveling for six years and have some time to go. It is time we get on with the task. He turned to Gene and me, asking, "Are the probes stored?" Gene and I confirmed it had been accomplished.

Buzz said, "Ok, let's get to the mission and find the God Particle. The course is laid in. Based on my calculations, we are almost halfway to our destination."

With a tired sigh, barely audible, "Let's be on our way."

He flipped his mic, saying, " OK, crew, you have five minutes to settle in your seats. We are getting out of here."

Buzz counted, three, two, one, and hit the rocket boosters. The sudden surge pressed us into our chairs as God Speed exited Uranus's gravity, and we were on our way.

It's midnight. I close with the following thoughts. We have traveled so far, doing science along the way. This has been a welcome distraction, for it could have been a monotonous transit. The team is anxious to get there. Thus far, the adventure has been full of excitement. I don't know what lies ahead but anxiously await the unknown.

As Shakespeare would say, "Once more unto the breach."

GOD PARTICLE CHASE BEGINS

May 11th 2050

Fifteen years have passed in the blink of an eye since we launched from Earth. God Speed has carried us through a remarkable odyssey across the cosmos. Our journey has taken us to Luna Colony on the Moon, where their pioneering efforts to establish a sustainable community have been nothing short of spectacular.

Humanity is rapidly advancing in its quest to colonize planets throughout the Galaxy. Luna Colony stands as the first successful step in living off-planet. Thanks to the revolutionary new element, Theonium-127, discovered by Theo and Vector, Luna Colony has built a fusion power plant capable of supporting a community of 10,000 people.

Just yesterday, I received an email from my friend Elmo, who shared the exciting news that Space Command has begun sending civilians to the Moon.

The prospect of visiting Luna on our return flight fills me with anticipation. Considering the time it will take to traverse the cosmos, I expect to see a thriving community when we arrive. I may be a little worse for wear, considering the years it will take for us to return. But I remain hopeful that Elmo and I will meet again.

Elmo has been on my mind frequently, and my feelings

for her have grown exponentially. We've been videoconferencing as often as possible.

Mars is thriving. The small team there is making significant strides, utilizing Theonium-127 for their fusion power plant, moving Mars closer to being habitable for larger communities.

Our exploration has taken us from Jupiter's unassuming expanse to Europa's breathtaking beauty. The Hermes adventure, landing and collecting samples, aims to discover whether Europa can sustain life.

Two days ago, we received word that Hermes had successfully arrived on Earth. Space Command is analyzing its data and has commenced developing plans to send scientists to establish an outpost on Europa within the next three years, for further exploration.

We have marveled at the beautiful but uninhabitable gas giant, Uranus. Each celestial stop is a testament to the wonders and mysteries of our solar system.

But now, as we hurtle through the darkness of interstellar space, the true vastness and desolation of the universe reveal themselves. Amidst the inky void, distant solar systems flicker like lighthouse beacons, teasing with the promise of discovery yet remaining tantalizingly out of reach.

Today, as we prepare to breach the cosmic speed of light and confront the enigmatic God Particle, a palpable mix of anticipation and trepidation fills the air.

We gathered in the briefing room, ready to discuss this long-awaited plunge into our mission: finding the God Particle. Gene and Juan, sitting to my right, were laughing with excitement, speculating about what we may find on the other side.

Gene said, "My guess is we will reach the speed of light and disintegrate. I have read all of the test data. There is a 15% chance we will not survive the acceleration. The expected G-force may exceed God Speed's structural integrity." She laughed and smiled, "Well, it will be so quick we will not have time to register it in our brains. We failed."

With a twinkle in his eye, Juan patted Gene on the shoulder and replied, "Have faith. Is that not what we are hoping for, God Particle?"

She nodded. Sipping her coffee, she turned and looked out the portal into the blackness of space, contemplating what may be.

Buzzed entered the room, exuding excitement, and began, "Good morning, everyone. Before we dive into today's preparations, I wanted to address Gene's speculation about our monumental endeavor. I've reviewed the data on the speed of light and understand the concerns. However, in my experience, test data often fails to capture the full scope of what will happen in the actual event. So, I've decided to disregard the data and focus on our strengths: a sound ship and a skilled crew. We're not just going to exceed the speed of light, we're going to survive and find the God Particle."

I glanced around the room and added, "Hell yes! We need to succeed, but let's also appreciate how far we've come. Look at the journey we've made. The colonies we've visited. Power plants we've enhanced. Saving the Bounty's crew. Europa would only be a theoretical endeavor had we not collected and sent data to Space Command. Even if this final mission doesn't go as planned, we should take pride in our accomplishments."

I laughed, finishing, "Assuming we survive."

Theo, with a sardonic laugh, chimed in, "I disagree. Finding the God Particle has always been our primary goal. All our detours and delays have been setbacks. None of our previous achievements will compensate for that failure if we fail now."

Vector, frowning, nodded in agreement with Theo's assessment.

Buzz raised his voice to regain control of the room. "Alright, everyone has had their say. Let's focus on tomorrow's task. I'll pilot God Speed through the speed of light once Juan initiates the propulsion drive. The rest of you will monitor your stations."

"Vector and Theo, keep a close watch on radiation levels; we're expecting spikes, though we hope they'll stay within the God Speed's protective limits."

Gene and Kelvin, your task is to look for anomalies: power spikes, energy readings, and radar signals that could indicate the presence of the God Particle."

If there's nothing else, let's get to preparing for tomorrow. We have a lot at stake, and it's time to ensure we're ready."

"Tomorrow promises to be a momentous leap into the unknown, where the very fabric of reality may be challenged. With resolve forged from the spirit of exploration, we press onward, ready to unravel the secrets that lie beyond the veil of stars."

As we draw closer to our goal, I feel as though I am truly seeing the beauty, wonder, and vastness of space for the first time. The sheer majesty of the cosmos stirs something deep within me, leading me to consider the possibility of a divine hand at work in this incredible creation.

We may find out tomorrow. Tonight, however, I anticipate a restless sleep, filled with the anxious anticipation of finally reaching our destination and facing whatever may lie ahead. Will the God Particle reveal its existence? Only time will tell.

Looking around the control center, it is late. As we finish our preparation, each crew member slowly migrates to their berths to contemplate tomorrow's adventure.

I'm off to my rack for a quick drink and hopefully some needed sleep. I wonder if this is the beginning or the end for God Speed and her crew.

BEGINNING OR END?

May 13th, 2050

I will attempt to recreate yesterday's events, though I am uncertain I can truly convey what we experienced.

The day began at 0700. A quiet and somber atmosphere enveloped the galley as the team gathered for breakfast. Each member sat lost in thought, contemplating their role in the upcoming experiment. Anticipation and worry were etched on their faces. Some had been part of the Hadro project before, witnessing failures and the loss of colleagues in the pursuit of understanding the universe. Others harbored doubts about the existence of God or any divine particle.

Theo and Vector exchanged weary glances, their minds replaying past experiences.

Equally burdened, others wore expressions of tentative hope, grappling with the weight of the mission. Silence lingered, broken only by the occasional clink of cutlery against plates, as the team braced itself for what lay ahead.

Buzz walked into the galley, a crucifix around his neck glinting under the lights, a testament to his Catholic faith. Gene glanced up, chuckled, and asked, "Do you really think that will protect you from what might happen today?"

In a deep, foreboding voice, Buzz smiled and replied, "We're venturing into the unknown. A bit of extra protection can't hurt. I trust that God will watch over us as we embark on this journey."

Gene smiled and nodded. "One can only hope for divine intervention if we're to succeed." Reflecting on her time as a Buddhist, she chuckled, "Perhaps I'll turn into a cow." This prompted laughter that broke the tension in the room.

The team began to discuss their assigned tasks and the procedures they needed to follow to achieve their goal.

By 0800, we had left the galley and settled into our designated stations, ready to collect data from this innovative and uncharted adventure.

Juan sat in his co-pilot's seat, staring at his instruments, mentally working through the procedures to engage the propulsion drive.

This drive is the first of its kind. Capable of pushing a ship beyond the speed of light. Concern and anxiety were etched on his face.

Sitting next to Juan in his pilot's seat, Buzz nervously reviewed the step-by-step documentation for piloting the craft as it approached the speed of light. He was responsible for implementing the emergency shutdown procedures.

Buzz turned to Juan, wide-eyed and filled with excitement and anxiety, laughed nervously, and said, "I hope these emergency procedures work. It has never been tested. I may blow us up."

Everyone within earshot laughed, as one does in a dangerous situation that may end in disaster. We were genuinely venturing into the unknown. Conventional wisdom holds that everything slows down as an object moves toward the speed of light. Theories also suggest that time itself may actually stop.

Theo, Vector, Gene, and I sat at our designated consoles, tightly strapped in, waiting for Juan to initiate the propulsion drive.

At precisely 0850 on May 12th, 2050, Juan looked over his shoulder at the team, a look of determination etched on his face, as he whispered, "Here we go." He glanced at each member, and in turn, with anxiety and excitement beaming from our faces, we each nodded, confirming we were ready.

Juan reached to his left and flipped the first of two toggle switches. I could feel the propulsion drive's first stage engage. A gentle rumble could be felt throughout God Speed. Looking around at the team, anticipation was etched on their faces. Juan said, "So far so good."

I realized that my breathing had quickened. I could feel my heart racing, anticipating the G-force we would soon feel as we achieved the speed of light. My mind raced, wondering whether we might be destroyed.

No human has ever traveled at the speed of light in the history of human space travel. I began to wonder if we could survive this.

Looking around the room, no one moved; we were lost in our thoughts, waiting for this monumental event to begin.

Excitement in his voice, Juan yelled over the propulsion drive's humming, "Here we go."

He flipped the switch. Activating the booster rocket. I heard a slight swish-like wind racing through a tunnel. Then, bang! We were violently thrown back into our seats. A force more significant than that experienced leaving Earth's gravitational pull.

Buzz monitored his console's instruments, reading out the speed changes as the craft propelled toward our goal. We were violently shaking in our seats. I felt as if my teeth would be jarred out of my head.

With clenched teeth and a muffled voice, Juan read out the G-force we felt as God Speed propelled us forward. At one point, in a high-pitched groan, he yelled, "We are at maximum G-force!"

Suddenly, a blinding light consumed the interior of the ship. Immediately, a peculiar sensation overtook me, as if my body was being stretched, reshaped, and distorted. I watched in awe as the faces of my team members twisted and contorted, their mouths hanging open in shock.

Each one seemed trapped in their own state of bewilderment. The scene reminded me of my childhood, watching taffy being pulled and stretched; a perfect analogy for the strange, elastic feeling I was experiencing.

Sitting there, surrounded by an alien, surreal environment, I struggled to comprehend my emotions. The blinding flash that had erupted around us was now replaced by an oppressive darkness. The ship felt suspended in time, with no sense of forward motion.

I heard Buzz take a deep breath, his voice filled with excitement and wonder. "We have gone beyond the speed of light. I think we have entered Transluminal space!" He declared.

His words were swallowed by the profound silence that followed as we grappled with the unending blackness that enveloped us.

Blackness so deep it swallows perception. It is the presence of silence itself. It presses inward, heavy, vast, and unbroken, a void that erases edges, shapes, and even the thought of distance. It is a silence so absolute it hums in your bones, not with sound but with its suffocating lack. Time seems suspended, dissolved into a stillness where breath feels too loud, heartbeats too intrusive. In that overwhelming blackness, there is no horizon, no anchor, only the infinite weight of emptiness wrapping around you, swallowing even the idea of escape.

A deep, unsettling foreboding hung in the air, a stark reminder of our isolation. I couldn't shake the thought: would we ever see light again?

As we began to gather our senses, conversations echoed through the ship's bleakness. We were all attempting to understand the unending darkness and how to move forward.

In a high-pitched voice, Gene asks, "Can anyone see anything. I feel as if I am blind. The blackness is complete, deprived of any light."

Each of us responded one by one, some in panicked voices: "I cannot see anything. Can you?"

Buzz's calm voice came over the radio, "Calm down, let's start figuring out how to get internal lighting back on."

With great relief, the ship's consoles began to light up, followed by all internal lighting. Buzz could access the piloting controls, and each team member could read their monitors.

I looked out into the abyss, squinting, straining to see anything. Suddenly, a tiny white light approached the ship's main viewing window. It grew in size as it quickly closed the distance. Our internal lights went dark. All consoles remained lit.

Slowly, we stood from our seats, staring in awe at this anomaly floating before us.
A thought came to me: "Is this a star that will consume us?"

It stopped and hovered near the ship. A bright celestial light flooded the cabin, surrounded by a calming blue hue. A warm feeling consumed me. Staring into this fantastic phenomenon, unfazed by its brightness, a sense of peace washed over me.

Observing my team members' expressions, I could see the light had the same effect on them. I have never felt so calm and at peace. I could hear the monitoring equipment's alarm bells blaring, but I could not do anything about it.

A vaguely familiar voice could be heard mumbling, "We have passed the speed of light." It was Buzz. I turned to my right, seeing an expression of wonder and bewilderment on his face. I can only imagine he saw the same expression on my visage.

At that moment, time seemed to stand still. We were

suspended in a timeless void, able to move only our heads, surrounded by surreal tranquility. The bending and reshaping of our bodies had stopped.

From my vantage point, looking out the port-side window, I beheld a breathtaking panorama of existence. I saw my life unfold before me from birth to the present moment. A being floated toward me, a female. Surprised and excited, I shouted, "It is my mother." The sound was immediately muffled. No one seemed to hear me. She smiled and nodded to me, a sight that felt humbling and awe-inspiring. I wonder if this is what is seen when we die?

She floated near me, her right arm outstretched, a gentle smile gracing her face as she turned and pointed.

In the distance, a small figure began to approach, growing more apparent with each passing moment. As it drew nearer, tears welled up in my eyes. The figure was a beautiful young girl with long blond hair and piercing blue eyes that captivated me. With a sudden cry of joy, I realized she was my daughter, her smile unmistakably familiar.

As she floated toward me, her voice was like a melody, "Hi, Daddy. I'm doing well. Know that there is life after death, and God will bring you to me."

She reached out, her hands tenderly cradling my face. A warmth of love enveloped me. Tears streamed down my cheeks as I wept with joy and wonder. I hadn't felt such peace and love in years.

Just as quickly as they had appeared, both vanished in the blink of an eye. Falling to my knees, I began to weep. The warmth and love were replaced with an all-encompassing emptiness. I struggled to comprehend what I had just experienced. Was it real? Had exceeding the speed of light triggered some anomaly in my brain, creating these vivid images? My mind whirled, attempting to make sense of this experience.

The encounter left me questioning everything. I desperately tried to regain that warm feeling of love and peace that had surrounded. A profound emptiness filled my entire being.

As quickly as the light appeared, darkness engulfed us. The vast expanse of emptiness and hopelessness returned, and dead silence consumed us.

Sitting in total darkness, I heard the computer's hard drives spinning as it strove to collect as much data as possible on this phenomenon. Little did I care.

Free from our paralyzes, the team scrambled to analyze the incoming data, revealing unprecedented levels of radiation and energy.

When out of the blackness, a glimmering orb approached. Behind the orb, a beautiful being rose.

We stared in stunned silence as the orb hovered before us, its glimmer casting a radiant glow that cut through the vast darkness of space. Upon it stood a being unlike anything we had ever known; its form shimmering with ethereal light, at once human in grace yet veiled in celestial mystery.

When it spoke, its voice was pure and melodic, resonating not in our ears but within our hearts.

"Welcome. Is this what you were searching for?"

The being extended its hands, presenting the orb. Energy pulsed within it, and streams of light raced across its surface, intertwining and bursting forth in near-blinding brilliance. Each flicker carried the weight of something immeasurable, something beyond comprehension.

Buzz glanced at Juan, whose eyes were wide in awe.

Vector, ever the scientist, was already reaching for his instruments, but even he seemed to hesitate. No one momentarily dared to break the silence, unsure of what to make of this extraordinary encounter.

Finally, I found my voice, stepping forward to address the being. "What… are you?"

The being met my gaze. Its eyes filled deep with knowledge, and it smiled serenely. "I am the keeper of what lies beyond. But it is not I who brought you here. It is your search for answers".

We were frozen, mesmerized by the overwhelming beauty. It smiled and, with a flash that momentarily blinded us, the orb and the being were gone. We were again in complete blackness.

In an instant, the tranquility was shattered. The craft shuddered violently. We were suddenly yanked back into standard space. The G-forces were crushing, making every breath a struggle. As I fought to stay conscious, a single thought flashed through my mind: "At least I got to see my daughter."

Silence enveloped us when the ship finally settled. Juan shut down the drive.

We sat, each lost in our thoughts, trying to comprehend what had happened. Time seemed meaningless in that void. I have no idea how long we had been hurtling beyond the speed of light. Where had we been? When had we been?

Stunned and disoriented, we lingered at our consoles, replaying the experience.

Eventually, we drifted from the control room to the galley, where we sat in deep contemplation.

Hours passed as we silently shared a meal, each of us lost in our thoughts, trying to grasp what we'd encountered. One by one, we finished eating and unconsciously made our way to our berths. Some crew sought solace in sleep, while others simply sat, replaying the events repeatedly in their minds.

As I close this entry, I'm left bewildered by what we experienced. Was it real, or just some bizarre anomaly triggered by breaking the light-speed barrier?

There's only one way to know for certain: We must return to Transluminal space, armed with the knowledge and insights from this first incursion. I want to see my daughter again.

Now, knowing what lies ahead, we'll be better prepared. But for now, I'm emotionally and intellectually drained. Sleep is what I need.

REVELATION

May 14th, 2050

    I woke this morning drained; my emotions frayed to the edge. Yesterday's wonder and confusion lingered like an echo, refusing to fade. Standing beneath the pulse of the sonic shower, I found myself mesmerized, my thoughts circling, unraveling, reforming, yet never settling. What had I truly experienced? Was it real, or only some fragile illusion I can't release?

    Walking into the galley, each team member sat alone, heads down, eating breakfast, stuck deep in their thoughts. Not one person lifted their head to see who entered. A heavy silence consumed the room. I heard a muffled grumble to my left. It was Theo. Only a few words could be heard. He said, "Is there…. Other lives…." He was not making sense.

    Buzz appeared, grabbed his usual eggs and bacon, sat beside me, smiled, and nodded. His expression was blank, devoid of any emotion.

    Finishing his meal, he stood and looked around the galley. His voice held a monotonous drone, a dull sound that mirrored his detached demeanor. "We need to get everyone moving. I know yesterday was difficult, and I guess each one of us has a story to tell. But first, we need to review the data. Let's see what we have." I could feel the team's lack of energy.

His words seemed to wake us from our melancholy. We slowly migrated from the galley into the control room. Each member moved into their console sets and began analyzing the data.

Sitting at my console, I looked around at each member methodically reviewing the data. My emptiness seemed to dissipate. Everyone wore the same expression: wonderment, confusion, and fear, as we mulled over the data. It suddenly struck me that each member must have had their own revelation during our time in Transluminal space. I thought, maybe, just maybe, we could share our God Particle adventure.

Late in the day, after all the data had been reviewed, we met to discuss our findings. As we gathered in the briefing room, Buzz spoke, "Okay, before we get to the analytics, I want to share what I experienced during yesterday's incursion."

He took a deep breath, his voice quivered, lacking his usual bravado, and began, "What happened yesterday was deeply unsettling. Right now, I cannot wrap my head around my experience. I believe it defies conventional science and logic. When we surpassed the speed of light and entered Transluminal space, I saw my life unfold before me."

"It was like watching a movie reel in fast-forward, every significant moment in my life, playing out before me. But then, I saw something more." Tears began to flow down Buzz's face. "The orb glowed, then a being bright and beautiful came toward me. As it got closer, its form became clearer. It was my father walking, maybe floating toward me."

"He passed away years ago. He began to speak. A beautiful melodic voice fills me with warmth and love. He told me he was proud of what I had achieved and would always watch over me."

"Before the image dissipated, my father reached out, touched my shoulder, smiled, and was gone. The warmth and love that poured into me were overwhelming. I fell to my knees, weeping. I did not want it to end. When he pulled away, the emptiness and darkness overwhelmed me."

His voice, at a whisper, continued, "It was otherworldly, too real to be a hallucination." Buzz bowed his head and sat down.

He paused, looked around the room, softly speaking, "I can see by the look on your faces that I wasn't the only one who had such an encounter. This wasn't just some physical phenomenon; it was deeply personal. I believe that orb, that being, was more than just energy or radiation. It was intelligent, sentient, maybe even divine."

The room was silent, everyone processing Buzz's words.

I stood and began speaking, "I saw my mother and daughter. My mother shone with a celestial glow, her smile overwhelming me with warmth and wonder, just as it had when I was a child."

"My daughter's long, beautiful blonde hair flowed behind her as if a gentle breeze were blowing. Her stunning blue eyes pierced my soul, and their radiant energy consumed me. My only thought was that I never wanted this feeling to leave me. My daughter said, 'Daddy, we are here waiting for you. Know that it is not too late for you. God will bring us together again."

Then, they both slowly faded, replaced by the blackness of the abyss, leaving me with cold and empty."

"I sat down and bowed my head, crying. I wondered if I would feel warmth again."

Gene cleared her throat, her face glowing with peace and

happiness. She spoke softly, "Throughout my life, I have searched for meaning. I've been an atheist, an agnostic, a Buddhist; nothing filled the emptiness inside me."

"Yesterday, I saw something. Was it God, an alien? I don't know. It showed me the possibilities in my life; all I must do is surrender. It didn't say how to accomplish this. I want to experience that feeling again."

Juan jumped in, "I saw Mrs. Flores, our village's curandero (medicine woman). Her dark black hair flowed, contracting the celestial light encompassing her. She stared into my soul with those dark brown eyes. Mesmerizing me. He said in a deep, commanding voice, 'Stay on the path with God. He does exist.' She pointed at the small ball of celestial light. 'That was created by God, who made the universe.' "Then she was gone. I was immobile for some time as the darkness consumed me."

With an expression of wonder, Juan laughed and, in a voice consumed with joy, said, "I had to travel millions of miles from home to have my curandero visit me, reminding me, as she had when I was a child, to stay on the right path." Grinning from ear to ear, he sat down.

Wearing a stern look, Theo turned to Vector, who mirrored his expression. "Vector, did you see anything?" he asked.

Vector slowly shook his head. Concern and what appeared to be some trepidation were evident on his face. He said, "I saw nothing but blackness, no light, no being. I heard screams of agony coming from the abyss. I have always known that nothing existed beyond this life, and this proves it." There was a small quiver in his voice.

Maybe he was reconsidering his position?

Theo nodded grimly. "I saw darkness, too, a deep nothingness that shook me to my core—a cold that no warmth could quench. I heard a small voice crying and instantly knew it was my mother. With deep sadness in her voice, she told me it wasn't too late to find the path."

Theo's voice trailed off, the weight of his words hanging heavily in the air. The room remained silent, each person lost in their own thoughts, contemplating the profound and unsettling experiences they had shared.

Buzz nodded, absorbing everyone's stories. He wondered out loud, "Was this a random event? Is it a message for us and the world? Maybe it is a message to the world that we must get out? What was the power emanating from the orb?"

He continued, "Setting aside the spiritual implications, we must dive deeper into the data. There has to be some clue supporting what happened and why."

"First, I must tell everyone about a strange occurrence. Last night, after our return from the abyss, and each of you meandered, deep in thought, to your berths. I realized I needed to write my report to Space Command. Sitting at my console, I noticed the incoming transmissions' database warning light flashing, indicating it was full. Selecting the most recent message, the computer announced, 'Message number 285, from Space Command, transmitted May 13th, 2052.'

"I hit the stop button, wondering if I had heard the receipt date correctly. I hit play again. The computer repeated the receipt date. Confused, I looked down at my watch; it displayed May 14th, 2050. A two-year variance. Believing my watch might have been damaged during the speed of light event, I quickly ran to the central nuclear clock on the pilot's console. It too displayed May 14th, 2050."

"Totally confounded, I decided to contact the Ares Haven. Pressing the radio transmission button, I began the call. A surprised voice came over the speaker, asking, 'Who is this? God Speed has not been heard from for two years. Provide the authentication code.'

"I provided God Speed's authentication code."

"Ares responded," 'God Speed, where have you been for the past two years? No one has been able to communicate with you. We concluded you must have perished when the speed of light propulsion drive was activated.'

"Now completely bewildered, I signed off with Ares Haven. Sitting at the control panel, contemplating this discovery, the only solution to confirm the unsettling news was to reach out to Space Command."

"I received the same response. Their authentication process took over an hour. Surprised and pleased that we were still alive, they asked where we had been for the past two years. I told them I had no idea and would spend the next few days with the team reviewing data to make sense of this conundrum."

"Space Command informed me that after one year with no communications from God Speed, they had designated us as lost in space. Our families were notified. That will be an interesting conversation; Space Command explaining their error."

Buzz continued, "So, I have speculated that what were hours to us beyond the speed of light appears to have consumed two years in real time space. This supports some theories that time stops at the speed of light. Let's see if we can prove it."

The briefing room erupted into chaos. Everyone spoke at once; confusion was evident on everyone's faces. Buzz held up his hand, saying, "Let's get started on the data. The answers we seek may lie in the details."

In silence, we shuffled out of the briefing room and back to our stations to continue the arduous task of reviewing the data.

We spent the last half of the day poring over the data. At midnight, realizing it would take days to digest our findings, we shut down for the night.

I will finish my whiskey and head to bed, anticipating what tomorrow will bring. This is a fantastic finding for any scientist. Two years lost are unsettling.

TRANSLUMINAL ENIGMA

May 18th, 2052 (or 2050), two years lost?

I woke this morning lying in my rack, deep in confused thought, unable to comprehend that we had lost two years of our lives.

Looking in the mirror, shaving, there was no evidence that I was two years older. I could not wrap my head around this realization. Here we were in space, isolated, our clocks reflecting a date two years earlier than the rest of Humanity. How was this possible? Did the aging process stop while in Transluminal space?

Contemplating this gave me a headache. Maybe we could find the answers as we dig through the data.

The entire immersion beyond the speed of light seemed to happen in the blink of an eye. One moment, we were on course, Buzz hit the propulsion drive, and bang, we were somewhere lost in time. Just as quickly, we were back in standard space. It was as if we had slipped into a dream state, woke disoriented, struggling to identify where we were—two years gone!

Four days had passed since our return from the unknown. The energy among the team in the galley was palpable. There was dead silence, all consumed in their thoughts about what had transpired. We devoured our breakfast, eager to find something in the data to explain what had happened to us.

We slowly migrated to our consoles. The room was thick with tension. Gene lifted her head from deep, introspective thoughts and voiced what everyone was feeling. "I cannot understand what happened," she said, her voice heavy with frustration. "My head aches, reliving the events in my mind. I cannot find any scientific or logical reasoning to explain what I experienced. There are only questions and no answers. Did we really lose two years? How was this possible? Can we find evidence proving the speed of light theory? Does time slow down or stop after achieving the speed of light? Did we see God?"

A murmur of agreement filled the room, a collective acknowledgment of the confusion and anxiety that had taken hold of the team. Gene's comments resonated deeply with everyone, encapsulating the uncertainty and profound mystery we were grappling with.

After poring over the data for four days, patterns began to emerge. The levels of radiation and energy from the orb were unlike anything we had ever encountered, almost as if it were a bridge between dimensions or realities. The orb's energy nature was unique, displaying characteristics of both matter and antimatter, suggesting it existed beyond our current understanding of physics.

One day flowed into another; we barely noticed. The data was fascinating, but it also raised more questions than answers.

Late today, Buzz called the team into the briefing room. He said, "We have spent the past many days reviewing all the data collected. I need your input. Space Command is requesting an update.

After a short silence, Gene said, "Based on my findings, I submit this energy could be linked to consciousness. The way it interacted with us, showing us our loved ones, it's as if it was tapping into our memories, our very souls."

Vector added, "If that's the case, it means there's a new field of physics we've just stumbled upon. One that connects the physical world with the metaphysical, maybe even the spiritual."

Buzz asks, "Vector, has your analysis and experience caused you to pause and rethink your belief that once we die, the cosmos just consumes our energy?"

Vector, with furrowed eyebrows, had no response.

Theo piped in with a scoff. "It is just energy. The energy readings I have seen are off the charts. If we can figure out how to harness it, we will have an infinite power supply for

Humanity. We need to go back into Transluminal space. I propose initiating the propulsion drive, getting past the speed of light again, and capturing the power source. Once collected, we can experiment with how best to utilize it."

Listening to each member's input, a thought occurred to me. Contemplatively, I said, "We need to consider another possibility. What if the being we saw is an alien? A living entity from another planet or galaxy. They are more advanced than Humanity. They may have the technology enabling them to delve into our consciousness. They accessed our memories that mean the most to us, and used them in an attempt to communicate with us?"

Juan was the last to speak, "Stop and think about the experience each of us had. I believe it was divine intervention. God has given Humanity what we have been looking for. Definitive proof God is present in all our lives."

Silence consumed the room for a few minutes. Vector looked at Theo, laughed, slapped him on the back, and said, "Well, Theo, how did it feel being next to God?"

Theo smiled sardonically and stood, saying, "If it is anything, I believe it is an alien life force with technology well beyond anything we can dream of.

Laughing, he bellowed, "Let's charge up the propulsion engine, go back into the abyss, and find God."

Buzz stood with a look of determination on his face. "I need to report our findings to Space Command. Based on this conversation, we have nothing substantial; more questions than answers. Without more substantial evidence, I cannot advise Command that we saw God, an alien, or nothing.

We need to know whether the orb is genuinely an unlimited power source. Can we harness it? Is there a being associated with the orb? Is it a superior alien power? If we go back through the speed of light, will we be in the same place, and can we contain and store the orb? How many years will we lose entering what I will call non-space?

With determination etched on our faces, we moved to our consoles and began the daunting task of finding scientific proof of what was beyond the speed of light.

Around 10:00 p.m., we met in the briefing room to discuss any additional findings. The consensus was that nothing additional had been learned. There was an air of disappointment in the room. Heads bowed, exhaustion was evident on everyone's faces.

Gene raised her head, and with frustration and fatigue in her eyes, she said, "We have pored over the data for days without finding concrete evidence to identify the orb or its source of power. What was the being we saw, and how do we explain what each of us experienced? I am overwhelmed trying to separate the emotions experienced from my logical mind. The only way to resolve this is by doing what we do best, science. We need to initiate the propulsion drive again and get into space beyond the speed of light."

She raised her voice with trepidation and frustration, saying, "We need to return! I need to go back!"

Theo stood, his voice quivering, and said, "I saw nothing but darkness. I need to know what is out there. There must be something I missed. Let's go!"

Vector, Juan, and I stood smiling and bellowed, "YES!"

Buzz said, "OK, first, I need to bring Space Command up to speed. I am all for another adventure, but first, let's see what Space Command has to say."

Later that evening, we sat in the galley passionately discussing our desire to dive back into Transluminal space. Sipping on whiskey, provided by the USS Bounty, only enhanced the energy in the room.

Buzzed walked in just as the uproar subsided. Looking around, with a tone of disappointment in his voice, he began, "I completed my briefing with Space Command. They expected more from this mission. I reminded them that, as with any science, trial and error are the watchwords."

"Space Command began ranting about the money expended on this mission and how many years it took to get to the heliosphere.

"Ignoring the rants, I informed them we were contemplating returning to Transluminal space. Our intention is to find and, if possible, bring back the orb for study."

"This was met with a definitive NO! I reminded them we needed to continue our mission to find the God Particle. We needed to go back. It's bigger than us. It could change the course of Humanity. This was met with silence."

Buzz continued, "Lastly, the Admiral told me, we had done all we could and it was time to come home. They have launched a new ship, Ariel (Lion of God), with a new science team. They are en route to assume this project and take it to the next level."

"I yelled at the Admiral. Informing him that the new team would take fifteen years to get here, and valuable time would be wasted. This was met with silence. I was ordered to compile the data and have recommended action plans available within the next few days. We are to forward the packets to Space Command and Ariel. We need to impart our combined knowledge on the mission to them."

An audible growl erupted in the room. Everyone shouted at once, their displeasure with Space Command's decision.

Buzz held up his arm, "We have done great work. We have aged fifteen years since the start of the project. It is our time to pass the torch and get back home. We should rendezvous with Ariel near Europa."

Each team member grumbled and stood, expressing their desire to proceed with a second incursion regardless of what Space Command had ordered.

Looking around the room, everyone wore the same expression of anger and exasperation. Sitting, sipping my whiskey, in a contemplative voice, causing everyone to pause and listen, I said, "Look, by the time we get back to Earth, if we make it, considering our age, most of us will be too old to care. So, let's go out with a bang. I submit we blow off Space Command and get to it! Let's flip the switch, dive back into Transluminal space, and figure this out. I don't know about you, but I must find out what was out there regardless of the cost. I want to feel the overwhelming love experienced, wherever we were."

Everyone jumped up with excitement, expressing their agreement with my recommendation.

Buzz scratched his head and smiled, "Well, it is late. We need to rest and consider what has been discussed. Tomorrow, we should complete the data packets and transmit them. Afterward, we will meet back here to discuss our options. Get some rest."

Lost in our own thoughts, we slowly migrated to our berthing areas.

As I lay here in my rack, my thoughts drifted back to the meeting with my mother and daughter. Their messages, appearance, and the warmth of love I felt brought calm back to me.

Whatever comes next, I feel a renewed sense of purpose. We are on the cusp of something incredible. I am ready to face it, knowing that we are not alone in our journey. My mind is made up. At the morning briefing, I will attempt to justify why this team should be the ones to go back into space beyond the speed of light.

CROSS ROADS

May 19th, 2052

Today, as we prepared to send our findings back to Earth, I couldn't help but feel a mixture of excitement and trepidation. We had encountered something extraordinary that challenged everything we knew about science and existence. It was a humbling reminder of how much there is still to discover and understand.

The encounter sparked existential questions about the nature of reality and the existence of a higher power. This left us with more questions than answers. Was this the God Particle? The genesis of the universe itself. Does God exist? Was the being an alien?

Standing at the galley entrance, I watched as the team went about their morning routine for breakfast. Buzz and Juan sat across the table, deep in an animated conversation. I could guess it was about whether to set a course for Mars or stay and complete the mission.

Theo and Vector were laughing at something Vector had said about Theo's breakfast.

Walking into the galley, the invigorating smell of freshly brewed coffee energized me. I quickly grabbed a cup and filled it to the brim, savoring the mesmerizing scent before taking a seat beside Gene.

She stared at her breakfast with a resolute conviction in her voice and said as if to herself, "I feel unsettled; we need to go back inside. We were the first. There are answers I must have."

She stood, raising her voice, and said, "We must be the ones! The one incursion left me empty. Did I experience a metaphysical event? Was it God?"

Everyone looked in Gene's direction. Dead silence consumed the galley.

Buzz slowly stood and began. "Alright, we need to discuss the elephant in the room. I have been ordered to set a course for Mars, then on to the Moon and Earth. As far as I can see, we have two options:

"One - do as ordered. Considering our current ages and the time it will take to return to Earth, most of us will either be too old to care or will not complete the return flight."

"Two - throw caution to the wind, disobey my orders, and go back and find out what is out there. I am driven by an almost uncontrollable desire to see that Being and Orb again. I need to satisfy the unanswered questions I have. To understand what was seen and felt."

"This is not a decision I will make on my own. I need a consensus. Should we engage the propulsion drive again to race through the speed of light, knowing that we may not survive this jump? Remember, we are the first to do this. Or turn tail and race home? I do not know whether the drive and ship will survive another incursion."

The tension in the room was almost visible as everyone absorbed Buzz's words. Gene, still reeling from being the center of attention, exchanged glances with the rest of the crew. The weight of the decision was clear on everyone's faces.

She smiled and said, "You already know my answer. I almost have an addict's illogical desire to get back into that space, see the orb, and harness it." She folded her arms and sat with a look of determination.

With a noticeable quiver in his voice, Theo said, "I need to face the darkness seen, hoping there will be more this time. I do not want to feel that emptiness and foreboding experience there. If nothing else, we can capture the orb and bring it back."

Vector stood angrily, "I do not want anything to do with that abyss. There is nothing out there. My vote is NO! We must consider our responsibilities and the risk to our lives."

Juan, the youngest crew member, set down his coffee cup, stood staring at Vector, and said, "But if we don't go back, won't we always wonder what could have been? I mean, isn't that part of why we're out here, to explore the unknown?" I say, yes, we should go. If we are to disobey an order, this should be the one."

With a tone of conviction, Buzz said, "OK, it is five to one for returning to Transluminal space. We have completed the data packets for Mars and Space Command. Juan and I will send them before the day is out. I recommend you ensure your equipment is ready for the incursion. Maybe prepare video recordings to include a Will for your families in case this goes sideways."

This decision seemed to lift everyone's spirits, except for Vector, who sat brooding in his seat.

There were no uncertainties. Energized by the decision, we went about our day preparing for tomorrow's incursion. Wills were made. Video messages created, and every piece of equipment inspected and made ready for this adventure.

After dinner, the team sat in the galley. A calm, soothing atmosphere could be felt within the room. There was no fear, no trepidation, just resolution. We were going. Everyone was drinking, sharing their tales from their last experience within the abyss. Some were hoping for more this time, while others were focusing on harnessing the energy. Juan hoped to have a conversation with the being that revealed itself.

The night wore on. We slowly migrated to our berthing, excited for tomorrow's adventure.

Reflecting on this journey, I cannot help but wonder: Did we genuinely glimpse the divine or merely scratch the surface of a universe brimming with mysteries yet to be unveiled? Time will tell. This experience has driven me to realize that I can no longer be an atheist. There is something greater than ourselves. The answer may be discovered tomorrow: good night, and Godspeed.

INCURSION

May 20th, 2052

I write this entry with a mixture of excitement and apprehension, hoping it will not be my last. It is 0700. While showering and shaving, images of the last encounter fill my mind. Will I see my daughter? My mother, the Orb? Will I be able to speak to the Being?

These questions surged through my mind like waves crashing onto a stormy shoreline.

As a side note, I still hate this sonic shower.

Assuming all goes well, I will add to this entry upon our return from the abyss. If I fail to return, my will is placed next to this journal, along with a farewell video. My excitement and anticipation are almost overwhelming. **Facta non verba!** (Deeds, not words!)

LOST

On February 1, 2065, the crew of the *USS Ariel* reached the edge of the heliosphere. During the fifteen-year transit, every attempt to raise God Speed had failed. Radio frequencies carried only static, and video channels returned nothing but black screens. The ship had gone silent, and *God Speed* had gone dark.

At Space Command, speculation turned to unease. Perhaps after that final transmission, the crew of *God Speed* had defied the order to return. Did they ignite their experimental propulsion system and hurled themselves past the light barrier, vanishing once more into transluminal space?

During the last conversation with God Speed, Buzz, the ship's captain, forcefully proclaimed his team had discovered the Orb. More power than humanity has ever seen. He had insisted he hand the crew had experienced "other worldly, spiritual events while in Transluminal space. He argued that his team should be the ones to again enter Transluminal space. Their experience gained in the first incursion made them the most qualified. Buzz's voice was passionate, hinting that God Speed crew would disregard orders.

God Speed had been ordered to return to Earth. En route, she was to rendezvous with the USS Ariel to brief them on the speed of light mission. Ariel would be the team that replaced God Speed and breached the speed of light for the second time.

Scotty O'Malley, Ariel's engineer, sat at his console, meticulously scanning for any sign of God Speed. After hours of traversing the heliosphere, Scotty's excited voice suddenly crackled over the radio to Max Anderson, the leader and pilot. "Max, I found her. She's adrift about three hundred kilometers off our port bow. I've scanned for life signs. There are none."

Max replied, "Roger that. Send me the God Speed location coordinates."

Entering Scotty's coordinates into the ship's navigation, Max increased the power and set a course for God Speed.

Fifteen minutes later, Ariel had reached its destination.

Max stood from his pilot's seat and walked to the observation port, the most forward part of the ship. He saw God Speed' gray shining hull, maintaining station as if it were crewed.

Sitting back down, Max reached for the ship's controls and steered Ariel 360 degrees around God Speed to inspect her for damage.

Max depressed the switch on his microphone and began recording his observations, "As I approach the craft from the port side, there is no visible structural damage to the hull. Traversing the remainder of the ship, all appears to be intact."

"Except for intermittent thruster bursts to maintain its programmed station, no fuel or gas leaks are visible. I will take a team on board to look for the crew and determine what may have happened."

Max turned off the recording device, reached for the ship's communications mic, and depressed the on switch. A green light displayed on his console indicated that the mic was on.

"Alright, Scotty," Max's voice came over the radio. "We need to board God Speed and find out what happened. Visually, she appears to be intact. There are no identifiable breaches or damage to the hull. Scotty, what did you find from your full diagnostics on their systems?"

Scotty replied, "All systems are fully operational, and nothing remotely out of sync. Engines are fine, oxygen levels are perfect, cabin pressure is correct, and environmental systems are up and running. Except for no crew, all is fine."

In a commanding voice, Max issued an order, "Scotty, meet me in the cargo bay and suit up. You and I will ingress to God Speed once on board. I will go to the bridge. You check the galley and crew berthing and head to the engine room. I will meet you there."

Scotty replied, "Roger. I just entered the cargo bay, suiting up and checking my equipment."

Max entered the cargo bay and climbed into his suit, his mind racing with questions. Is the crew lying dead on board? If so, how did they die? Is the ship empty? Where did the crew go? Did they initiate the propulsion drive?

Max and Scotty walked to the decompression chamber. The last to enter, Scotty grabbed the hatch handle and slowly closed it behind them. A metallic sound reverberated within the chamber. A hissing sound flowed, confirming the hatch had sealed tightly and was releasing the pressure within the chamber. Looking above the exit hatch, a red light flashed, indicating it was not yet safe to open the outer door. After a few minutes, the light blazed green, confirming it was safe to open the hatch and exit.

Max opened the outer hatch, exposing them to the darkness of space. Buzz smiled in wonderment as he floated in the darkness, surrounded by the awesomeness of shining stars. He shouted into the abyss, "This is amazing."

Scotty lifted his left arm and flipped a flap, exposing a tracking device. A red dot on the tracking device displayed the location of God Speed. Looking in the direction they must travel, Scotty spoke into his mic, "Max, we need a heading of 050 degrees to get to God Speed."

Their suits were equipped with propulsion units, allowing them to control their trajectory. Within twenty minutes, they reached God Speed, ready to confront whatever awaited them.

Max arrived first at the main hatch to enter Godspeed. He turned toward Scotty, who had just arrived, and smiled. "I am not sure what we will find," he said. "Be prepared."

Entering the ship, Max continued, "It just dawned on me that the crew may have died because of age. Consider this: the crew's average age was thirty-five when they left Earth. It took fifteen years to arrive, making them roughly fifty. We took another fifteen years to get here, so if they are alive, they are ancient."

"Scotty chuckled with a nostalgic glint in his eyes. 'Well, in a few years, that'll be us. But let's not forget what happened to the *God Speed*. Space Command's last communication with the ship came on May 18th, 2052. The directive given God Speed was clear: head back to Earth and rendezvous with us en route. After that day, complete silence. Neither Space Command nor the colonies received any further signals."

With great effort, Max turned the main access handle; the external hatch of God Speed creaked open. Both men floated inside, the metallic clang echoing in the confined space. Max sealed the outside hatch behind them.

Scotty quickly located the access panel in the chamber and began the pressurization process. He pressed the green button labeled "Pressurize Chamber." A soft hiss filled the space as the pressure balanced with the main cabin's. The subtle vibrations of the chamber and the sharp creaking of cold metal filled their senses.

A green light flickered on above the entrance hatch, bathing the room in a reassuring glow. Scotty glanced at Max, whose eyes reflected relief and excitement. With a nod, Scotty turned the handle on the entrance hatch. The door swung open with a low groan, revealing the interior of God Speed.

Inside, the dim lights gradually brightened, casting a soft glow over the sleek controls and advanced technology that lined the walls. The gentle hum of the ship's systems was almost comforting. Max could feel a sense of purpose building as they stepped into the ship's cockpit.

Except for the ship's power center humming, the ship was devoid of life.

Max lifted his left arm, and with his right arm, he depressed his communication button, enabling him to communicate to Ariel, saying, "Albert, this is Max; we have safely entered God Speed and will begin our search and analysis."

Albert Holmes, one of two scientists on board, replied, "Roger, let us know if you need something. We are receiving your location beacons and can see exactly where you are on the ship. Out."

Max and Scotty heard a computer voice over the internal communications, "Pressure is equalized; it is safe to remove your protective gear."

Max pulled off his headgear, removed the propulsion pack, sat on the deck, and called out, "Is anyone on board?" His voice echoed throughout the ship, and an eerie feeling came over him. He became unnerved by the echo and silence within the ship, and his heart raced. Sweat droplets slid down the back of his neck as he and Scotty walked toward the control room, fearing they would find deceased crew members.

Looking around, nothing seemed out of place except for some dust on the deck. The gear is stored correctly, and nothing is loose lying around. The panels on the bulkhead displayed all pertinent internal environmental information: oxygen at 99%, temperature 75, and humidity a comfortable 60%.

Turning into the control room, Max wondered whether they would see bodies in their seats. To his relief, the room was empty. Max walked to the main control panel and sat down to begin performing a complete diagnostic.

Turning to Scotty, he said, "I have this. Go through the galley and berthing area. See if you can find anyone or clues as to what may have happened. Then, head to engineering. Determine what condition the main engine is in. Next, check their propulsion drive. It may give us clues as to when it was last initiated."

Scotty smiled nervously, saying, "I will do that. This is really creepy. There is no damage to the ship, and everything seems to be functioning properly. Did they vanish?" He glanced at the empty chairs, his brow furrowed. "Do you think they tried to breach the speed of light again? If so, what happened?"

Looking into the distance, Scotty said, "I wouldn't blame them if they went again. While en route to relive them, I took the opportunity to read their personal logs and review the data. I would have wanted another shot at it, too.

Imagine experiencing something so profound and not knowing if it was real. They did lose two years, after all."

Max turned away from the console, looked at Scotty, and sternly said, "Are you done? Let's get moving on this. We need to figure out what happened and fast. If they've succeeded, they could be anywhere in time or space. And if they failed….."

To Max's left, the meters displayed the status of lighting, environmental systems, and engine functionality, reflecting all systems operating within normal ranges. The center monitors were operating correctly, displaying various areas throughout the ship.

Max flipped a switch to his right labeled "outside cameras." The display lit up. He could see all sections of the ship's port side. With the toggle switch, he changed the display to show other ship sections. After spending thirty minutes inspecting the outer hull, with a satisfied expression, Max nodded to himself and turned off the monitor.

Scotty moved out of the control room and down the corridor, walking twenty feet to the next hatch. It was the galley. Glancing around, he saw nothing out of place. Four tables centered in the room, with chairs neatly tucked underneath, all clean.

Turning to his left, he walked into the main kitchen area. The stove, microwave ovens, and refrigerators were spotless.

Opening the refrigerator, it took all of his willpower to keep from vomiting. The rotten smell wafting from the spoiled vegetables and meat on the racks was overwhelming. He grabbed the gallon of milk from the top shelf. He didn't need to open it to determine it was spoiled. As he grabbed it, he felt thick sludge sloshing inside the container. This was another sign that something had gone wrong, but what?

Scotty radioed Max, saying, "I just completed checking out the galley. Everything is neat and clean. The only sign of an issue is the spoiled food in the fridge. I am no expert, but I guess that months, maybe years, have passed since the food was placed in there. There is mold everywhere within the fridge. I am moving on to the berthing area. I am hoping not to see dead bodies. I feel strange that someone is here, but the place is empty. All this silence is playing with my mind."

Max chuckled at the comment and responded, "Just stay on task. I am finished here; I will meet you in the berthing area."

Scotty turned to his right as he exited the galley. Walking down the empty passageway, he called back to Max, "It is dead silent here. Unnerving." He quickly came upon the berthing hatch and slowly opened it. His face filled with anguish, anticipating seeing the crew dead in their racks.

Standing in the open hatch, looking around the berthing area, hesitating to enter. Suddenly, Scotty felt someone grab his shoulder. With wide eyes and surprise, Scotty closed his fists and turned, prepared to defend himself. As he turned swinging, Max grabbed Scotty's arm, laughing, yelling, "What the heck are you doing? Did you think I was a ghost or an alien?"

Sheepishly, Scotty looks into Max's eyes. You scared the crap out of me. You could have announced yourself."

With a nod, Max released Scotty's arm. They walked into the Berthing. It was a typical ship's berthing. Each crew member had personal space with a small door for privacy. Looking into each room, there was no evidence anyone had been in the space for some time. Each rack is perfectly made—the clothing is properly stored. Not one article of clothing was out of place. On each of the crew's desks adjacent to their rack, personal photos and a handwritten letter were found, signed, and placed at the center of the desk. Each had a video next to the letter.

Max read each letter, realizing it was addressed to a family member. The date inscribed on all letters was the same: May 20, 2052. Max mumbled, "Hm, the day after the last communications with God Speed. That is not a coincidence."

It was as if the members were saying their last farewells. Each letter started with the same two sentences, "Today we embark on an adventure. This letter is written in case something goes sideways, precluding us from returning from the abyss."

Speaking as if within himself, Max said, "This supports the idea that God Speed's team decided to go back into the abyss. But what went wrong?"

After thoroughly inspecting the berthing area and finding nothing significant, Max and Scotty headed for engineering.

Walking into engineering, the steady hum of the power plant was comforting.

"Well, at least this is normal," Scotty muttered. "The plant and main engines are running properly."

He moved to the central control console, fingers gliding across the panels with practiced precision. For the next thirty minutes, he ran a full diagnostic sweep, the room filled only with the soft whir of systems responding to his commands.

Finally, he turned to Max.

"Both the power plant and engine are working at peak performance. Looking at the engine's data, whatever happened, the main engine was not put under any undue stress."

Scotty pointed to the front of the engine room, where the propulsion drive sat, emitting a soft, almost celestial blue hue. A look of concern showed on Scotty's face, and he said, "We need to check out the propulsion drive."

Max turned with caution in his voice, "Well, let's get to it." Leading the way, they cautiously walked toward the propulsion drive's control panel.

Standing over the control panel, Scotty noted, "First, whatever this glow is, it is not emitting any radioactivity. The data reflects the drive's last engagement, May 20th, 2052. The day after, God Speed was directed to head home."

Max ask, "Is there a shutdown date?

Scotty continued, "It is odd. According to the design manuals, if the drive had initiated a launch, there should have been a corresponding return date. There is not one. It could be that the God Speed team is lost somewhere in time."

Max responded, "No return date? What do you think the celestial blue hue is?

Scotty wrinkled his face, shrugged his shoulders, and replied, "I have no idea. The glow has never been identified nor experienced anywhere in the documentation, my training, or simulations."

He turned away from the console, smiled uncertainly, and said, "Well, let's walk to the drive and see what we see?

Max's mind spun as both men slowly and cautiously walked toward the drive. His thoughts raced: What might happen to them if they touched the drive? Will they be lifted up to the unknown? Will they be vaporized?

Shaking his head, freeing himself from the thought. He found himself standing directly in front of the propulsion drive. There was a warm, calming Ora around it. Max looked at Scotty, who was staring at the drive, mesmerized by the glow.

Max reached out, grabbed Scotty by the arm, and shook him, bringing him back from his internal thoughts.

Scotty asks, "Ok, what now?"

Max smiled, reflecting uncertainty. He looked at Scotty as he bent down, slowly moving his right arm toward the drive, nervously saying, "Well, let's see what happens." He closed his eyes as his arm moved closer. The hand quickly passed through the blue hue with no effect.

Scotty winced, expecting something disastrous or wonderful to happen.

Max stood, removed his hand from the drive, held it up for Scotty to see, and laughed, saying, "Nothing. The drive felt both cool and warm, but other than that, nothing."

Both men began a thorough physical inspection of the drive. Neither could find any anomalies.

Max looked at Scotty and said, "Let's get back to Ariel. I need to report our findings and see what Space Command wants to do next."

Within thirty minutes, Max and Scotty had returned to Ariel.

Max completed composing his report. He walked into the control room, sat in his seat, leaned back in the chair, and took a deep breath. Staring out into space, he gathered his thoughts about God Speeds.

He began reliving his walk through the emptiness of God Speed, unable to truly comprehend what had transpired. It unnerved him: a completely intact, perfectly functioning craft without its crew—just gone.

Doubt began to bubble to the surface of Max's mind, wondering whether his team should assume the mission to engage their propulsion drive. His thoughts were flooded with questions, asking himself, "If we engage the drive, will we be lost, too? Will we find the God Speed crew? Is the God Speed crew in a different universe we cannot see? If they are there, can they see us, and are they striving to communicate with us? Is the risk worth the reward?"

Scotty had been shaking Max on his shoulder for the past few minutes. Scotty asked, "Boss, are you alright"?

As if waking from a dream, Max nodded, flipped the video communication switch, and said, "Space Command, this Ariel comes in."

A few minutes later, Space Command responded, "Roger, this is Space Command. Stand by for the Admiral."

A familiar face could be seen. Max recognized his old boss with a glowing smile. "Hello, Max. This is Admiral Jackson. How have you been, my friend?"

Max responded, "It is great to see you, Sir. How is the family?

The Admiral smiled and said, "Max, they are well, Elizabeth, and I were just talking about you and this adventure yesterday."

Max continued, "Sir, our trip has been uneventful until now. We arrived and found God Speed. My engineer and I boarded with no problems. Our inspection of the outer hull before boarding revealed the ship was in perfect condition. No evidence of damage. The main control room was our first stop. After reviewing all available data at the consoles, I confirmed everything was normal. The ship's navigation system was on target, and the ship was precisely where it should be. Notably, the last course adjustment recorded in the log was dated May 20th, 2052—the day after your final communications with God Speed."

"Curiously, ten minutes after God Speed arrived at this current location, the entire ship, including the engines, power supplies, and environmental equipment, was switched to computer control mode. As you know, a ship configured this way can function independently until the engine fails and power is depleted. Otherwise, the computer will remain on station until instructed otherwise."

"Despite the ship's perfect condition, the crew is missing. The silence was eerie, our footsteps echoing as we walked about the ship. We searched for any sign of the crew or clues about their fate."

Our last stop was engineering, which was operating flawlessly on autopilot. The last item we checked was the propulsion drive. Looking at its console, I noticed it had May 20th, 2052, as an execution date, but no return date."

"Sir, as you know, if an incursion beyond the speed of light has been accomplished, and since the ship is here, a return date should be displayed on the console."

"After our ingress, we have no real answer for the missing crew. Only questions."

"My science team and engineer convened to discuss the unusual situation regarding the ship. We struggled to understand how the ship could be here without the crew. Each team member applied their expertise, meticulously analyzing the data collected to determine what might have happened."

"The data supports God Speed initiated the drive, as evidenced by the launch date on the console. The team made some assumptions - God Speed entered Transluminal space and somehow separated the team from the ship during the incursion. Only the ship returned. It is as if something extracted the crew and returned the ship empty. We cannot find a scientific explanation to support such an anomaly. Our consensus is that we must initiate our propulsion drive, enter Transluminal space, and see if we can locate the God Speed team."

"Sir, we do have some reservations about using the drive. Assuming the incursion into the abyss caused God Speed's team to be lost, we worry our fate will be the same."

Before Max could continue reporting, Admiral Jackson interrupted. In a deep, forceful voice, the Admiral yelled,

"Captain Anderson! I do not want to discuss your crew's concerns." "They volunteered for this mission. By 1000 hours tomorrow, you and your crew will initiate your propulsion drive. Now you go find God Speed's mission crew!"

With a stern look, Max stood and saluted the Admiral, replying, "Yes, sir. "But…" The Admiral had cut off the transmission.

Max nodded to himself, turned in his seat away from the video console, grabbed his microphone, clicked on the internal communications switch, grumbling, and said, "Team, meet me in the briefing room in five minutes!"

Maxed raised himself from his seat and bowed his head in great concentration, struggling to break the news to the team. On his way to the briefing room, he stopped in the galley to grab a cup of coffee. He sat sipping his favorite columbine brew, contemplating a strategy for getting the team on board for their incursion into the abyss.

Suddenly, it hit him. His team had spent countless hours preparing for this mission. With a satisfied nod to himself, he grabbed his coffee, stood, and confidently walked to the briefing room.

The team was assembled when they entered the briefing room. Scotty sat at the far end of the table, sipping his mango smoothly, with a concerned and knowing look on his face. Max nodded to him as if to say, "Scotty, yes, we are going into the abyss."

The astrophysicists Albert Holmes and Danti Sagan sat to Max's left, discussing their theories on God Speed team's disappearance.

Max, still standing, slowly looked from one team member to another, attempting to read their mood. Before he could say anything, Scotty stood with a resolved look and said, "We are going to initiate the propulsion unit and head into the unknown?"

Max responded, "Yes. Space Command has ordered us to initiate the drive by 1000 hours tomorrow. Albert and Danti go to your consoles and complete a diagnostic of all monitoring equipment. I do not want to miss collecting data as we jettison through the speed of light. Scotty, you and I will check the propulsion drive and run a quick simulation to ensure it is ready for initiation."

With a twinkle in his eye, Albert stood and, before leaving, gleefully said, "Let's do it! All this time in space, now we get to do science. No theorizing, no postulating, action! I am ready to travel into the unknown."

Danti looked around the room, frowned, crossed himself, looked to the sky, and said, "God protect us."

INTO THE ABYSS

February 2nd, 2065

Max woke from a restless sleep. He quickly jumped into the sonic shower and dressed. His mind raced in anticipation of today's adventure. Looking into the mirror, he smiled, saying, "We will succeed on this mission." With this newfound resolve, he made his way to the control room.

Max took a deep breath, feeling the moment's weight as he stepped further into the control room. The hum of the ship's systems and the soft, rhythmic tapping of Scotty's console created an almost tangible sense of anticipation. He nodded to Scotty, who acknowledged him with a brief, focused glance before returning to his preparations.

Max turned to face Danti and Albert, seated to his left. Danti's eyes sparked with excitement. "Let's do this, boss," Danti said, his voice brimming with energy. "I'm excited to see what's on the other side. I've always believed something greater than ourselves created the universe. Let's go meet it. God, alien, supreme power, whatever it is."

Max smiled, feeling the gravity of Danti's words and the shared sense of purpose among the crew. "We're about to leap into the unknown," he said, his voice steady. "Whatever awaits us, we'll face it together. Let's make history."

The room buzzed with anticipation and anxiety. Crew members nodding and exchanging determined glances. Final system checks were completed.

Scotty reported that all drive systems were fully primed. The control room's lights dimmed slightly, and glowing console screens cast a futuristic, almost ethereal ambiance over the space.

Scotty looked up, giving Max a thumbs-up. "Everything's ready, Captain."

Max took his position at the central command console, his heart racing with nerves and excitement. In a command voice, Max said, "Initiate the drive."

Scotty's fingers danced over the controls; the ship shuddered gently, the familiar hum escalating into a resonant thrum. The control room lights flickered momentarily as the ship prepared to enter the unknown. Max looked around at his crew, each face reflecting a mixture of awe and determination.

The countdown began. Each second stretching into an eternity of collective breath-holding. Suddenly, the entire ship began to pitch and shake out of control. Then, dead silence. Scotty's console lit up with warning lights. Alarms began to blare. Everyone turned to Scotty, looking for answers.

With confusion in his voice, Max asks. "What's going on?"

Scotty shouted, "The fire suppression unit has activated in the propulsion drive compartment!" His voice edged with urgency.

Scotty and Max leaped from their seats and sprinted without hesitation toward the propulsion drive compartment. As he darted out of the room, Max yelled over his shoulder to Danti and Albert, "Check the other systems! Make sure nothing else is compromised!"

Danti and Albert reviewed the ship's systems. Nothing else on the ship had been affected.

Danti flipped the communications switch at his console and reported to Max, "Sir, we have completed the diagnostics on all other systems. Everything is functioning properly."

Max responded, "Roger."

Danti and Albert sat at their consoles, patiently waiting for a report on what had happened.

Entering the drive compartment, relief spilled over Max's face as he observed that the fire suppression and ventilation systems had done their job. The fire was out, and no smoke was present within the compartment.

Scotty ran to the propulsion drive. A look of exasperation filled his face. Kneeling down to inspect the drive, he saw a large three-foot by a six-inch split in the center, with steam slowly emanating as if it was its last gasp before dying.

Max walked to the drive, touched Scotty's shoulder, and whispered, "My god, it is destroyed. Can it be fixed?"

Scotty slowly rose, turned to Max, shaking his head, and said sadly, "Short of an intervention by God, it is done."

They slowly traced their steps back to the control room. Hearing Scotty and Max reentering, Danti and Albert turned from their work to see the disappointment on their faces.
 In a defeated voice, Max said, "The drive is done. The mission is a failure before it starts. What do you have to report?"

Danti replied, "All systems are functioning properly except for the propulsion drive."

Max walked slowly with his head bowed to his seat and sat. He took a deep breath and reached for the switch to initiate video communications with Space Command. As if speaking to himself, he said, "This is one call I wish I did not have to make."

He flipped the switch and called, "Space Command, this is Ariel. Come in."

A few seconds later, Admiral Jackson, with a stern look,

came into focus. Angry, he said, "Captain, what are you calling for? You are to have initiated the drive and jumped through the speed of light!"

With disappointment evident in his voice, Max bowed his head and replied, "Sir, at 1000 hours, we initiated the propulsion drive. It engaged, and then an anomaly occurred. The ship's fire suppression was initiated. When entering the drive's compartment to investigate, we discovered a three-foot by six-inch crack in the drive. It is not reparable."

The silence was overwhelming; it felt as if the oxygen had been sucked out of the room.

After what seemed like forever, the Admiral stood from his chair, screaming, "What! How could this happen? We have no way to search for God Speed's crew! It is an utter failure."

Max slowly spoke. "Sir, we have sent all the data to you. Our pre-initiation procedures were followed to the letter. We found no anomalies in the drive. We have yet to review the data to determine what may have caused the catastrophic destruction."

After a long, uncomfortable silence, Admiral Jackson sat back in his chair, grinding his teeth, and said, "Alright, Max, we will review the data to ensure this will not happen again.

Now, as for you, I am ordering you and your team to head home. There is nothing more that can be done."

He frowned and softly spoke with sadness in his eye, "As for God Speed, we will have to suspend the search until we can get another team out there with a new drive."

Max responded, "Sir, I have a better solution. Let my team board God Speed and use its drive."

The Admiral quickly snapped, "NO! Leave the ship where it sits. The auto controls are engaged, and she has sufficient power to maintain the station for twenty-plus years. On the off chance that this phenomenon may reverse itself, we need to keep God Speed on station."

Max replied, "Roger, sir, we will begin our return course no later than tomorrow."

Max flipped the video switch to the "off" position, disconnecting communication with Space Command. He looked at the team and said, "Okay, let's go home."

GOD SPEED – AN UNANSWERED QUEST

February 3rd, 2065. As Ariel turns on her course home, Buzz watches God Speed slowly slip from view. He wonders aloud, "Will we ever discover what happened?"

"Farewell, my friend."

AUTHOR:

DOUGLAS SERVED 20 YEAR IN THE UNITED STATES NAVY. FATHER OF 4 GIRLS AND 1 SON, 10 GRANDCHILDREN AND 3 GREAT GRANDCHILDREN.

E-MAIL: DLRENDERBOOKS@GMAIL.COM

www.ingramcontent.com/pod-product-compliance
Lightning Source LLC
Chambersburg PA
CBHW050025180626
46810CB00002B/571